The Doom of London by Fred M White

Fred Merrick White was born in 1859 in West Bromwich in the Midlands of England to Joseph White and Helen Merrick who had married the previous year.

Joseph was a solicitor's managing clerk, who by the time the family moved to Hereford a few years later, had become a solicitor's article clerk.

Little is known of White's early years but what is known is that he followed in his father's footsteps and worked as a solicitor's clerk in Hereford. His father by now had also become a solicitor and times seemed quite prosperous for the family.

However in the late 1880's something went badly wrong for his father and he was imprisoned.

White had by now decided that writing was a more preferable career for him than the law. By 1891 Fred M. White, now 31 years old, was working full-time as a journalist and author, earning enough to support himself and his mother, Helen. By this time Fred's younger brother, Joseph A. White, had left home and working as a glass-blower.

In 1892, White married Clara Jane Smith. The wedding took place at King's Norton, Worcestershire, and the couple went on to have two children; Sydney Eric White (1893) and Ormond John White (1895).

As the century closed Fred's father had been released from prison and was living as a "retired solicitor", together with Helen, in Worthington in West Sussex.

By the time of the 1911 census, Fred M. White, now 52 years old, and his wife Clara were living at Uckfield, a town in the Wealden district of East Sussex. As the ominous shadows of the First World War gathered White had established himself as a popular and extremely prolific author. Indeed whether it was novels or short stories they flowed from his pen with a startling speed and many of them were initially serialized in the popular weekly and monthly magazines. His clever use of science to create imaginative and highly adventurous story lines was a particular talent of his.

During the First World War, both of his sons served as junior officers in The Royal Inniskilling Fusiliers.

The titanic struggle of the First World War and his sons' war-time experiences in it greatly influenced this phase of his writing. His novel The Seed of Empire (1916), describes early trench warfare in great and gritty detail. He went on to describe how the social changes after the war created many problems for returning soldiers as they attempted to fit back into a now peaceful society.

Fred and Clara spent their twilight years in Barnstaple in Devon, an area which also provided the backdrop for his novels The Mystery Of Crocksands, The Riddle Of The Rail, and The Shadow Of The Dead Hand.

Fred Merrick White died in Barnstaple in 1935.

Index of Contents

THE FOUR WHITE DAYS

I

The editor of The Daily Chat wondered a little vaguely why he had come down to the office at all. Here was the thermometer down to 11O with every prospect of touching zero before daybreak, and you can't fill a morning paper with weather reports. Besides, nothing was coming in from the North of the Trent beyond the curt information that all telegraphic and telephonic communication beyond was impossible. There was a huge blizzard, a heavy fall of snow nipped hard by the terrific frost and—silence.

To-morrow—January 25th—would see a pretty poor paper unless America roused up to a sense of her responsibility and sent something hot to go on with. The Land's End cables often obliged in that way. There was the next chapter of the Beef and Bread Trust, for instance. Was Silas X. Brett going to prove successful in his attempt to corner the world's supply? That Brett had been a pawnbroker's assistant a year ago mattered little. That he might at any time emerge a penniless adventurer mattered less. From a press point of view he was good for three columns.

The chief "sub" came in, blowing his fingers. The remark that he was frozen to the marrow caused no particular sympathy.

"Going to be a funeral rag to-morrow," the editor said curtly.

"That's so," Gough admitted cheerfully. "We've drawn a thrilling picture of the Thames impassable to craft—and well it might be after a week of this Arctic weather. For days not a carcase or a sack of flour has been brought in. Under the circumstances we were justified in prophesying a bread and meat famine. And we've had our customary gibe at Silas X. Brett. But still, it's poor stuff."

The editor thought he would go home. Still he dallied, on the off chance of something turning up. It was a little after midnight when he began to catch the suggestion of excitement that seemed to be simmering in the sub-editor's room. There was a clatter of footsteps outside. By magic the place began to hum like a hive.

"What have you struck, Gough?" the editor cried.

Gough came tumbling in, a sheaf of flimsies in his hand.

"Brett's burst," he gasped. "It's a real godsend, Mr. Fisher. I've got enough here to make three columns. Brett's committed suicide."

Fisher slipped out of his overcoat. Everything comes to the man who waits. He ran his trained eyes over the flimsies; he could see his way to a pretty elaboration.

"The danger of the corner is over," he said, later, "but the fact remains that we are still short of supplies; there are few provision ships on the seas, and if they were close at hand they couldn't get into port with all this ice about. Don't say that London is on the verge of a famine, but you can hint it."

Gough winked slightly and withdrew. An hour later and the presses were kicking and coughing away in earnest. There was a flaming contents bill, so that Fisher went off drowsily through the driving snow Bedford Square way with a feeling that there was not much the matter with the world after all.

It was piercingly cold, the wind had come up from the east, the steely blue sky of the last few days had gone.

Fisher doubled before the wind that seemed to grip his very soul. On reaching home he shuddered as he hung over the stove in the hall.

"My word," he muttered as he glanced at the barometer. "Down half-an-inch since dinner time. And a depression on top that you could lie in. Don't ever recollect London under the lash of a real blizzard, but it's come now."

A blast of wind, as he spoke, shook the house like some unreasoning fury.

II

It was in the evening of the 24th of January that the first force of the snowstorm swept London. There had been no sign of any abatement in the gripping frost, but the wind had suddenly shifted to the east, and almost immediately snow had commenced to fall. But as yet there was no hint of the coming calamity.

A little after midnight the full force of the gale was blowing. The snow fell in powder so fine that it was almost imperceptible, but gradually the mass deepened until at daybreak it lay some eighteen inches in the streets. Some of the thoroughfares facing the wind were swept bare as a newly reaped field, in others the drifts were four or five feet in height.

A tearing, roaring, blighting wind was still blowing as the grey day struggled in. The fine snow still tinkled against glass and brick. By nine o'clock hundreds of telephone wires were broken. The snow and the force of the wind had torn them away bodily. As far as could be ascertained at present the same thing had happened to the telegraphic lines. At eleven o'clock nothing beyond local letters had been delivered, and the postal authorities notified that no telegrams could be guaranteed in any direction outside the radius. There was nothing from the Continent at all.

Still, there appeared to be no great cause for alarm. The snow must cease presently. There was absolutely no business doing in the City, seeing that three-fourths of the suburban residents had not managed to reach London by two o'clock. An hour later it became generally known that no main line train had been scheduled at a single London terminus since midday.

Deep cuttings and tunnels were alike rendered impassable by drifted snow.

But the snow would cease presently; it could not go on like this. Yet when dusk fell it was still coming down in the same grey whirling powder.

That night London was as a city of the dead. Except where the force of the gale had swept bare patches, the drifts were high—so high in some cases that they reached to the first floor windows. A half-hearted attempt had been made to clear the roadways earlier in the day, but only two or three main roads running north and south, and east and west were at all passable.

Meanwhile the gripping frost never abated a jot. The thermometer stood steadily at 15O below freezing even in the forenoon; the ordinary tweed clothing of the average Briton was sorry stuff to keep out a wind like that. But for the piercing draught the condition of things might have been tolerable. London had experienced colder weather so far as degrees went, but never anything that battered and gripped like this. And still the fine white powder fell.

After dark, the passage from one main road to another was a real peril. Belated stragglers fought their way along their own streets without the slightest idea of locality, the dazzle of the snow was absolutely blinding. In sheltered corners the authorities had set up blazing fires for the safety of the police and public. Hardly a vehicle had been seen in the streets for hours.

At the end of the first four and twenty hours the mean fall of snow had been four feet. Narrow streets were piled up with the white powder. Most of the thoroughfares on the south side of the Strand were mere grey ramparts. Here and there people could be seen looking anxiously out of upper windows and beckoning for assistance. Such was the spectacle that London presented at daybreak on the second day.

It was not till nearly midday of the 26th of January that the downfall ceased. For thirty six hours the gale had hurled its force mercilessly over London. There had been nothing like it in the memory of man, nothing like it on record. The thin wrack of cloud cleared and the sun shone down on the brilliant scene.

A strange, still, weird London. A white deserted city with a hardy pedestrian here and there, who looked curiously out of place in a town where one expects to see the usual toiling millions. And yet the few people who were about did not seem to fit into the picture. The crunch of their feet on the crisp snow was an offence, the muffled hoarseness of their voices jarred.

London woke uneasily with a sense of coming disaster. By midday the continuous frost rendered the snow quite firm enough for traffic. The curious sight of people climbing out of their bedroom windows and sliding down snow mountains into the streets excited no wonder. As to the work-a-day side of things that was absolutely forgotten. For the nonce Londoners were transformed into Laplanders, whose first and foremost idea was food and warmth.

So far as could be ascertained the belt of the blizzard had come from the East in a straight line some thirty miles wide. Beyond St. Albans there was very little snow, the same remark applying to the South from Redhill. But London itself lay in the centre of a grip of Arctic, ice-bound country; and was almost as inaccessible to the outside world as the North Pole itself.

There was practically no motive power beyond that of the underground railways, and most of the lighting standards had been damaged by the gale; last calamity of all, the frost affected the gas so that evening saw London practically in darkness.

But the great want of many thousands was fuel. Coal was there at the wharfs, but getting it to its destination was quite another thing. It was very well for a light sleigh and horse to slip over the frozen snow, but a heavily laden cart would have found progression an absolute impossibility. Something might have been done with the electric trams, but all overhead wires were down.

In addition to this, the great grain wharfs along the Thames were very low. Local contractors and merchants had not been in the least frightened by the vagaries of Mr. Silas X. Brett; they had bought "short," feeling pretty sure that sooner or later their foresight would be rewarded.

Therefore they had been trading from hand to mouth. The same policy had been pursued by the small "rings" of wholesale meat merchants who supply pretty well the whole of London with flesh food. The great majority of the struggling classes pay the American prices and get American produce, an enormous supply of which is in daily demand.

Here Silas X. Brett had come in again. Again the wholesale men had declined to make contracts except from day to day.

Last and worst of all, the Thames—the chief highway for supplies— was, for the only time in the memory of living man, choked with ice below Greenwich.

London was in a state of siege as close and gripping as if a foreign army had been at her gates. Supplies were cut off, and were likely to be for some days to come.

The price of bread quickly advanced to ninepence the loaf, and it was impossible to purchase the cheapest meat under two shillings per pound. Bacon and flour, and such like provisions, rose in a corresponding ratio; coal was offered at "2 per ton, with the proviso that the purchaser must fetch it himself.

Meanwhile, there was no cheering news from the outside—London seemed to be cut off from the universe. It was as bad as bad could be, but the more thoughtful could see that there was worse to follow.

III

The sight of a figure staggering up a snow drift to a bedroom window in Keppel Street aroused no astonishment in the breast of a stolid policeman. It was the only way of entry into some of the houses in that locality. Yet a little further on the pavements were clear and hard.

Besides, the figure was pounding on the window, and burglars don't generally do that. Presently the sleeper within awoke. From the glow of his oil stove he could see that it was past twelve.

"Something gone wrong at the office?" Fisher muttered. "Hang the paper! Why bother about publishing the Chat in this weather?"

He rolled out of bed, and opened the window. A draught of icy air caught his heart in a grip like death for the moment. Gough scrambled into the room, and made haste to shut out the murderous air.

"Nearly five below zero," he said. "You must come down to the office, Mr. Fisher."

Fisher lit the gas. Just for the moment he was lost in admiration of Gough's figure. His head was muffled in a rag torn from an old sealskin jacket. He was wrapped from head to foot in a sheepskin recently stripped from the carcase of an animal.

"Got the dodge from an old Arctic traveller," Gough explained. "It's pretty greasy inside, but it keeps that perishing cold out."

"I said I shouldn't come down to the office to-night," Fisher muttered. "This is the only place where I can keep decently warm. A good paper is no good to us—we shan't sell five thousand copies to-morrow."

"Oh, yes, we shall," Gough put in eagerly "Hampden, the member for East Battersea is waiting for you. One of the smart city gangs has cornered the coal supply. There is about half a million tons in London, but there is no prospect of more for days to come The whole lot was bought up yesterday by a small syndicate, and the price to-morrow is fixed at three pounds per ton—to begin with. Hampden is furious."

Fisher shovelled his clothes on hastily. The journalistic instinct was aroused.

At his door Fisher staggered back as the cold struck him. With two overcoats, and a scarf round his head, the cold seemed to draw the life out of him. A brilliant moon was shining in a sky like steel, the air was filled with the fine frosty needles, a heavy hoar coated Gough's fleecy breast. The gardens in Russell Square were one huge mound, Southampton Row was one white pipe. It seemed to Gough and Fisher that they had London to themselves.

They did not speak, speech was next to impossible. Fisher staggered into his office and at length gasped for brandy. He declared that he had no feeling whatever. His moustache hung painfully, as if two heavy diamonds were dragging at the ends of it. The fine athletic figure of John Hampden, M.P., raged up and down the office. Physical weakness or suffering seemed to be strangers to him.

"I want you to rub it in thick," he shouted. "Make a picture of it in to-morrow's Chat. It's exclusive information I am giving you. Properly handled, there's enough coal in London to get over this crisis. If it isn't properly handled, then some hundreds of families are going to perish of cold and starvation. The State ought to have power to commandeer these things in a crisis like this, and sell them at a fair price— give them away if necessary. And now we have a handful of rich men who mean to profit by a great public calamity. I mean Hayes and Rhys-Smith and that lot. You've fallen foul of them before. I want you to call upon the poorer classes not to stand this abominable outrage. I want to go down to the House of Commons to-morrow afternoon with some thousands of honest working-men behind me to demand that this crime shall be stopped. No rioting, no violence, mind. The workman who buys his coals by the hundredweight will be the worst off. If I have my way, he won't suffer at all—he will just take what he wants."

Fisher's eves gleamed with the light of battle. He was warm now and the liberal dose of brandy had done its work. Here was a good special and a popular one to his hand. The calamity of the blizzard and the snow and the frost was bad enough, but the calamity of a failing coal supply would be hideous. Legally, there was no way of preventing those City bandits from making the most of their booty. But if a few thousand working-men in London made up their minds to have coal, nothing could prevent them.

"I'll do my best," Fisher exclaimed. "I'll take my coat off to the job—figuratively, of course. There ought to be an exciting afternoon sitting of the House to-morrow. On the whole I'm glad that Gough dragged me out."

The Chat was a little late to press, but seeing that anything like a country edition was impossible, that made little difference Fisher and Gough had made the most of their opportunity. The ears of Messrs. Hayes Co. were likely to tingle over the Chat in the morning.

Fisher finished at length with a sigh of satisfaction. Huddled up in his overcoat and scarf he descended to the street. The cold struck more piercingly than ever. A belated policeman so starved as to be almost bereft of his senses asked for brandy—anything to keep frozen body and soul together. Gough, secure in his grotesque sheep skin, had already disappeared down the street.

"Come in," Fisher gasped. "It's dreadful. I was going home, but upon my word I dare not face it. I shall sleep by the side of my office fire to-night."

The man in blue slowly thawed out. His teeth chattered, his face was ghastly blue.

"An' I'll beg a shelter too, sir," he said. "I shall get kicked out of the force. I shall lose my pension. But what's the good of a pension to an officer what's picked up frozen in the Strand?"

"That's logic," Fisher said sleepily. "And as to burglars—"

"Burglars! A night like this! I wish that the streets of London were always as safe. If I might be allowed to make up the fire, sir—"

But Fisher was already asleep ranged up close alongside the fender.

IV

The uneasy impression made by the Chat special was soon confirmed next morning. No coal was available at the wharves under three shillings per hundredweight. Some of the poorer classes bought at the price, but the majority turned away, muttering of vengeance, and deeply disappointed.

Whatever way they went the same story assailed them. The stereotyped reply was given at King's Cross, Euston, St. Pancras and in the Caledonian Road. The situation had suddenly grown dangerous and critical. The sullen, grotesque stream flowed back westward with a headway towards Trafalgar Square. A good many sheepskins were worn, for Gough's idea had become popular.

In some mysterious way it got abroad that John Hampden was going to address a mass meeting. By half past two Trafalgar Square and the approaches thereto were packed.

It was a little later that Hampden appeared. There was very little cheering or enthusiasm, for it was too cold. The crowd had no disposition to riot, all they wanted was for the popular tribune to show them some way of getting coal—their one great necessity—at a reasonable price.

Hampden, too, was singularly quiet and restrained. There was none of the wildness that usually accompanied his oratory. He counselled quietness and prudence. He pledged the vast gathering that before night he would show a way of getting the coal. All he required was a vast orderly crowd outside St. Stephen's where he was going almost at once to interrogate Ministers upon the present crisis. There was a question on the paper of which he had given the President of the Board of Trade private notice. If nothing came of that he would know how to act.

There was little more, but that little to the point. An hour later a dense mass of men had gathered about St. Stephen's. But the were grim and silent and orderly.

For an ordinary afternoon sitting the House was exceeding full. As the light fell on the square hard face of John Hampden a prosy bore prating on some ubiquitous subject was howled down. A minute later and Hampden rose.

He put his question clearly and to the point. Then he turned and faced the modestly retiring forms of Mr. John Hayes and his colleague Rhys-Smith, and for ten minutes they writhed under the lash of his bitter invective. As far as he could gather from the very vague reply of the Board of Trade representative, the Government were powerless to act in the matter. A gang of financiers had deliberately chosen to put money in their pockets out of the great misfortune that had befallen London. Unless the new syndicate saw their way to bow to public opinion—

"It is a business transaction," Hayes stammered. "We shall not give way. If the Government likes to make a grant to the poorer classes—"

A yell of anger drowned the sentence. All parts of the House took part in the heated demonstration. The only two cool heads there were the Speaker and John Hampden. The First Lord rose to throw oil on the troubled waters.

"There is a way out of it," he said presently. "We can pass a short bill giving Parliament powers to acquire all fuel and provisions for the public welfare in the face of crises like these. It was done on similar lines in the Dynamite Bill. In two days the bill would be in the Statute Book—"

"And in the meantime the poorer classes will be frozen," Hampden cried. "The Leader of the House has done his best, he will see that the bill becomes law. After to-night the working-people in London will be prepared to wait till the law gives them the power to draw their supplies without fear of punishment. But you can't punish a crowd like the one outside. I am going to show the world what a few thousands of resolute men can accomplish. If the two honourable members opposite are curious to see how it is done let them accompany me, and I will offer them a personal guarantee of safety."

He flung his hand wide to the House; he quitted his place and strode out. Hayes rose to speak, but nobody listened. The dramatic episode was at an end, and Hampden had promised another. Within a few minutes the House was empty. Outside was the dense mass of silent, patient, shivering humanity.

"Wonderful man, Hampden," the First Lord whispered to the President of the Board of Trade; "wonder what he's up to now. If those people yonder only knew their power! I should have more leisure then."

V

Outside the House a great crowd of men, silent, grim, and determined, waited for Hampden. A deep murmur floated over the mass as those in front read from Hampden's face that he had failed so far as his diplomacy was concerned.

His obstinate jaw was firmer, if possible, there was a gleam in his deep-set eyes. So the greedy capitalists were going to have their pound of flesh, they were not ashamed to grow fat on public misfortune.

Hampden stood there by the railings of Palace Yard and explained everything in a short, curt speech.

Only those who were in need of coal were present. But there would be others to-morrow and the next day and so on. Then let them go and take it. The thing must be done in a perfectly orderly fashion. There were huge supplies at King's Cross, Euston, St. Pancras, in Caledonian Road, amply sufficient to give a couple or so of hundredweight per head and leave plenty over for the needs of others. Let them go and take it. Let each man insist upon leaving behind him a voucher admitting that he had taken away so much, or, if he had the money, put it down there and then at the usual winter's rate per hundredweight. The method would be of the rough rule of thumb kind, but it would be a guarantee of honesty and respectability. There were but few military in London, and against a force like that the police would be perfectly powerless. It was to be a bloodless revolution and a vindication of the rights of men.

A constable stepped forward and touched Hampden on the shoulder. Most of those near at hand knew what had happened. Hampden had been arrested for inciting the mob to an illegal act. He smiled grimly. After all, the law had to be respected. With not the slightest sign of hostility the great mass of people began to pass away. With one accord they turned their faces to the North. The North—Western district was to be invaded.

"Case for bail, I suppose?" Hampden asked curtly.

"Under certain conditions, sir," the inspector said. "I shall have formally to charge you, and you will have to promise to take no further part in this matter."

Hampden promised that readily enough. He had done his part of the work so that the rest did not signify. He was looking tired and haggard now, as well he might, seeing that he had been sitting up all night with some scores of labour representatives planning this thing out. He made a remark about it to Fisher who was standing by, mentally photographing the great event.

Then he fastened upon Hampden eagerly, "I want all the details," he said. "I wasn't so foolish as to regard this thing as quite spontaneous. You must have worked like a horse."

"So we have," Hampden admitted. "Fact is, perils that might beset Londoners have long been a favourite speculative study of mine. And when a thing like this—be it famine, flood, or an Arctic winter— comes we are certain to be the mark of the greedy capitalist. And I knew that the Government would be powerless. Fuel, or the want of it, was one of the very early ideas that occurred to me. I found out where—the big supplies were kept, and pretty well what the normal stock is. I pigeon-holed those figures. You can imagine how useful they were last night. There are some two hundred officials of Trades Unions with yonder orderly mob, and every one of them knows exactly where to go. There will be very little crowding or rioting or confusion. And before dark everybody will have his coal."

Fisher followed with the deepest interest.

"Then you are going to leave the rest to your lieutenants?" he asked.

"I'm bound to. In a few minutes I shall be on my way to Bow Street. Inciting to robbery, you know. No, there is no occasion to trouble—a hundred men here will be willing to go bail for me. If I were you I should have been somewhere in the neighbourhood of King's Cross by this time."

Fisher nodded and winked as he drew his sheepskin about him. He wore a pair of grotesque old cavalry boots, the tops of which were stuffed with cotton wool. A large woollen hood, such as old Highland women wear, covered his head and ears. There were many legislators similarly attired, but nobody laughed and nobody seemed to be in the least alive to the humours of the situation.

"Come along," Fisher said to Gough, who was trying to warm the end of his nose with a large cigar. "Seems a pity to waste all this album of copy upon a paper without any circulation."

"What would have a circulation in this frost?" Gough growled. "How deserted the place is! Seems shuddering to think that a man might fall down in Trafalgar Square in the broad daylight and die of exposure, but there it is. Hang me if the solitude isn't getting on my nerves."

Gough shivered as he pulled his sheepskin closer around him.

"This is getting a nightmare," he said. "We shall find ourselves dodging Polar bears presently. It isn't gregarious enough for me. Let's get along in the direction where Hampden's friends are."

VI

Meanwhile the vast mob of London's workers was steadily pressing north. There were hundreds of carts without wheels, which necessarily hampered the rate of progression, but would save time in the long run, for there were any number up to a dozen with each conveyance, seeing that various neighbours were working upon the co-operation system.

Gradually the force began to break and turn in certain directions. It became like an army marching upon given points by a score or more of avenues. It was pretty well known that there were a couple of hundred men amongst the multitude who knew exactly where to go and who had instructions as to certain grimy goals.

They were breaking away in all directions now, quiet, steady, and determined, covering a wide area from Caledonian Road to Euston, and from Finsbury Park to King's Cross. They were so quiet and orderly that only the crunch of the snow and the sound of heavy breathing could be heard.

Near Euston Station the first sign of resistance was encountered. A force of eighty police barred the way. The mob closed in. There was no hot blood, no more than grim determination with a dash of sardonic humour in it. A head or two was broken by the thrashing staves, but the odds were too great. In five minutes the whole posse of constables was disarmed, made secure by their own handcuffs and taken along as honoured prisoners of war. Perhaps their sympathies were with the mob, for they made nothing like so fine a fight of it as is usually the case.

Up by King's Cross Station a still larger force of police had massed, and here there was some considerable amount of bloodshed. But there were thousands of men within easy distance of the fray, and the white silence of the place became black with swaying figures and the noise of turmoil carried far. Finally the police were beaten back, squeezed in between two vastly superior forces and surrendered at discretion.

The victory was easier than it seemed, for obviously the constables had no heart for the work before them. Not a few of them were thinking of their own firesides, and that they would be better off in the ranks of their antagonists.

Meanwhile, many of the local municipalities were being urged to call out the military. With one accord they declined to do anything of the kind. It was the psychological moment when one touch of nature makes the whole world akin. In the House of Commons, to the agonised appeal of Hayes and his partner, the Secretary for War coldly preferred to be unable to interfere unless the Mayor of this or that borough applied for assistance after reading the Riot Act. The matter was in the hands of the police, who would know how to act upon an emergency.

Hustled and bustled and pushed good-naturedly, Fisher and his colleague found themselves at length beyond a pair of huge gates that opened into a yard just beyond Euston Station. There was a large square area and beyond three small mountains of coal, all carefully stacked in the usual way. Before the welcome sight the stolid demeanour of the two thousand men who had raided the yard fairly broke down. They threw up their hands and laughed and cheered. They stormed the office of the big coal company, who were ostensible owners of all that black wealth, and dragged the clerks into the yard. From behind came the crash and rattle of the wheel-less carts as they were dragged forward.

"No cause to be frightened," the man in command explained. "We're here to buy that coal, one or two or three hundredweight each, as the case may be, and you can have your money in cash or vouchers, as you please. But we're going to have the stuff and don't you forget it. You just stand by the gates and check us out. You'll have to guess a bit, but that won't be any loss to you. And the price is eighteen pence a hundredweight."

The three clerks grinned uneasily. At the same moment the same strange scene was being enacted in over a hundred other coalyards. Three or four hundred men were already swarming over the big mound, there was a crash and a rattle as the huge blocks fell, the air was filled with a grimy, gritty black powder, every face was soon black with it.

Very soon there was a steady stream away from the radius of the coal stacks. A big stream of coal carts went crunching over the hard, frozen snow pulled by one or two or three men according to the load, or how many had co-operated, and as they went along they sang and shouted in their victory. It was disorderly, it was wrong, it was a direct violation of the law, but man makes laws for man.

Gough and Fisher, passing down parallel with Euston Road, presently found themselves suddenly in the thick of an excited mob. The doors of a wharf had been smashed in, but in the centre of the yard stood a resolute knot of men who had affixed a hose pipe to one of the water mains and defied the marauders with vigorous invective. Just for a moment there was a pause. The idea of being drenched from head to foot with a thermometer verging upon zero was appalling. These men would have faced fire, but the other death, for death it would mean, was terrible.

"Does that chap want to get murdered?" Fisher exclaimed. "If he does that, they will tear him to pieces. I say, sir, are you mad?"

He pressed forward impulsively. Mistaking his intention, the man with the hosepipe turned on the cock vigorously. A howl of rage followed. But the dramatic touch was absent, not one spot of water came. A sudden yell of laughter arose in time to save the life of the amateur fireman.

"The water is frozen in the mains," a voice cried.

It was even as the voice said. In a flash everything became commonplace again. Fisher was very grave as he walked away.

"This is a calamity in itself," he said. "The water frozen in the mains! By this time to-morrow there won't be a single drop available."

VII

Inside the House a hot debate was in progress on the following day. Martial law for London had been suggested. It was a chance for the handful of cranks and faddists not to be neglected. It was an interference with the liberty of the subject and all the rest of it. The debate was still on at ten o'clock when Fisher came back languidly to the Press gallery. At eleven one of the champion bores was still speaking. Suddenly an electric thrill ran through the House.

The dreary orator paused—perhaps he was getting a little tired of himself. Something dramatic had happened. There was the curious tense atmosphere that causes a tightening of the chest and a gripping of the throat before actual knowledge comes. Heedless of all decorum, a member stood behind the Speaker's chair, and called aloud:

"The Hotel Cecil is on fire!" he yelled. "The place is well a-blaze!"

Fisher darted from the gallery into the yard. Even the prosy Demosthenes collapsed in the midst of his oration, and hurried out of the House. There was no occasion to tell anybody what the magnitude of the disaster meant. Everybody knew that in the face of such a disaster the fire brigade would be useless.

In the Strand and along the approaches thereto, along the Embankment and upon the bridges, a dense mass of humanity had gathered. They were muffled in all sorts of strange and grotesque garments, but they did not seem to heed the piercing cold.

In the Strand it was as light as day. A huge column of red and white flame shot far into the sky, the steady roar of the blaze was like surf on a stony beach. There was a constant crackle like musketry fire.

The magnificent hotel, one of the boldest and most prominent features of the Strand and the Thames Embankment, was absolutely doomed. Now and then the great showers of falling sparks would flutter and catch some adjacent woodwork but all the roofs around were covered with firemen who beat out the flames at once. Tons of snow were conveyed up the fire escapes and by means of hastily rigged up pullies, so that gradually the adjacent buildings became moist and cool. But for this merciful presence of the snow, the south side of the Strand from Wellington Street to Charing Cross might have passed into history.

As it was now, unless something utterly unforeseen occurred, the great calamity had been averted. There was still much for the firemen to do.

"Let's get back to the office," Fisher said, with chattering teeth. "I would sell my kingdom for a little hot brandy. I hope the next blizzard we get we shall be more prepared for. I suppose that out in the States they would make nothing of this. And we haven't got a single snow plough worthy of the name this side of Edinburgh."

"We are ready for nothing," Gough grumbled. "If there had been a wind to-night, nothing could have saved the Strand. The disaster may occur again; indeed, there is certain to be a fire, half-a-dozen fires, before daybreak. Given a good stiff breeze and where would London be? It makes one giddy to think of it."

Gough said nothing. It was too cold even to think. Gradually the two of them thawed out before the office fire. A languid sub came in with a pile of flimsies. Quite as languidly Gough turned them over. His eyes gleamed.

"My word," he gasped. "I hope this is true. They've had two days' deluge in New York. We are to keep our eyes open for strong Westerly gales with a deep depression—"

For the next two hours Fisher bent over his desk. The room seemed warmer. Perhaps it was the brandy. He took off his sheepskin and then his overcoat below. Presently a little bead of moisture grew on his forehead. He drew a little further from the fire. He felt stifling and faint, a desire for air came over him.

A little doubtful of his own condition he almost shamefacedly opened the window. The air was cold and fresh and revived him, but it was not the steely, polished, murderous air of the last few days. Somebody passing over the snow below slipped along with a peculiar soaking soddened sound.

Fisher craned his head out of the window. Something moist fell on the nape of his neck. He yelled for Gough almost hysterically. Gough also was devoid of his overcoat.

"I thought it was fancy," he said unsteadily.

Fisher answered nothing. The strain was released, he breathed freely. And outside the whole, white, silent world was dripping, dripping, dripping...

THE FOUR DAYS' NIGHT

I

The weather forecast for London and the Channel was "light airs, fine generally, milder." Further down the fascinating column Hackness read that "the conditions over Europe generally favoured a continuance of the large anti-cyclonic area, the barometer steadily rising over Western Europe, sea smooth, readings being unusually high for this time of the year." Martin Hackness, B.Sc., London, thoughtfully read all this and more. The study of the meteorological reports was part of his religion almost. In the laboratory at the back of his sitting-room were all kinds of weird-looking instruments for measuring sunshine and wind pressure, the weight of atmosphere and the like. Hackness trusted before long to be able to foretell a London fog with absolute accuracy, which, when you come to think of it, would be an exceedingly useful matter. In his queer way Hackness described himself as a fog specialist. He hoped some day to prove himself a fog-disperser, which is another word for a great public benefactor.

The chance he was waiting for seemed to have come at last. November had set in, mild and dull and heavy. Already there had been one or two of the dense fogs under which London periodically groans and does nothing to avert. Hackness was clear-sighted enough to see a danger here that might some day prove a hideous national disaster. So far as he could ascertain from his observations and readings, London was in for another dense fog within the next four-and-twenty hours.

Unless he was greatly mistaken, the next fog was going to be a particularly thick one. He could see the yellow mists gathering in Gower Street, as he sat at his breakfast.

The door flew open and a man rushed in without even an apology. He was a little man, with sharp, clean-shaven features, an interrogative nose and assertive pince-nez. He was not unlike Hackness, minus his calm ruminative manner. He fluttered a paper in his hand like a banner.

"It's come, Hackness," he cried. "It was bound to come sometime. It's all here in a late edition of the Telegraph. We must go and see it."

He flung himself into an armchair.

"Do you remember," he said, "the day in the winter of 1898, the day that petroleum ship exploded? You and I were playing golf together on the Westgate links."

Hackness nodded eagerly.

"I shall never forget it, Eldred," he said, "though I have forgotten the name of the ship. She was a big iron boat, and she caught fire about daybreak. Of her captain and her crew not one fragment was ever found."

"It was perfectly still and the effect of that immense volume of dense black smoke was marvellous. Do you recollect the scene at sunset? It was like looking at half-a-dozen Alpine ranges piled one on the top of the other. The spectacle was not only grand, it was appalling, awful. Do you happen to recollect what you said at the time?"

There was something in Eldred's manner that roused Hackness.

"Perfectly well," he cried. "I pictured that awful canopy of sooty, fatty matter suddenly shut down over a great city by a fog. A fog would have beaten it down and spread it. We tried to imagine what might happen if that ship had been in the Thames, say at Greenwich."

"Didn't you prophesy a big fog for to-day?"

"Certainly I did. And a recent examination of my instruments merely confirms my opinion. Why do you ask?"

"Because early this morning a fire broke out in the great petroleum storage tanks, down the river. Millions of gallons of oil are bound to burn themselves out—nothing short of a miracle can quench the fire, which will probably rage all through to-day and to-morrow. The fire-brigades are absolutely powerless—in the first place the heat is too awful to allow them to approach; in the second, water would only make things worse. It's one of the biggest blazes ever known. Pray Heaven, your fog doesn't settle down on the top of the smoke."

Hackness turned away from his unfinished breakfast and struggled into an overcoat. There was a peril here that London little dreamt of. Out in the yellow streets newsboys were yelling of the conflagration down the Thames. People were talking of the disaster in a calm frame of mind between the discussion of closer personal matters.

"There's always the chance of a breeze springing up," Hackness muttered. "If it does, well and good, if not—but come along. We'll train it from Charing Cross."

A little way down the river the mist curtain lifted. A round magnified sun looked down upon a dun earth. Towards the South-east a great black column rose high in the sky. The column appeared to be absolutely motionless; it broadened from an inky base like a grotesque mushroom.

"Fancy trying to breathe that," Eldred muttered. "Just think of the poison there. I wonder what that dense mass would weigh in tons. And it's been going on for five hours now. There's enough there to suffocate all London."

Hackness made no reply. On the whole he was wishing himself well out of it. That pillar of smoke would rise for many more hours yet. At the same time here was his great opportunity. There were certain experiments that he desired to make and for which all things were ready.

They reached the scene of the catastrophe. Within a radius of five hundred yards the heat was intense. Nobody seemed to know the cause of the disaster beyond the general opinion that the oil gases had ignited.

And nothing could be done. No engine could approach near enough to do any good. Those mighty tanks and barrels filled with petroleum would have to burn themselves out.

The sheets of flame roared and sobbed. Above the flames rose the column of thick black smoke, with just the suspicion of a slight stagger to the westward. The inky vapour spread overhead like a pall. If Hackness's fog came now it meant a terrible disaster for London.

Further out in the country, where the sun was actually shining, people watched that great cloud with fearsome admiration. From a few miles beyond the radius it looked as if all the ranges of the world had been piled atop of London. The fog was gradually spreading along the South of the Thames, and away as far as Barnet to the North.

There was something in the stillness and the gloom that London did not associate with ordinary fogs.

Hackness turned away at length, conscious of his sketchy breakfast and the fact that he had been watching this thrilling spectacle for two hours.

"Have you thought of a way out?" Eldred asked. "What are you going to do?"

"Lunch," Hackness said curtly. "After that I propose to see to my arrangements in Regent's Park. I've got Grimfern's aeroplane there, and a pretty theory about high explosives. The difficulty is to get the authorities to consent to the experiments. The police have absolutely forbidden experiments with high explosives, fired in the air above London. But perhaps I shall frighten them into it this time. Nothing would please me better than to see a breeze spring up, and yet on the other hand—"

"Then you are free to-night?" Eldred asked.

"No, I'm not. Oh, there will be plenty of time. I'm going with Sir Edgar Grimfern, and his daughter to see Irving, that is if it is possible for anyone to see Irving to-night. I've got the chance of a lifetime at hand, but I wish that it was well over, Eldred my boy. If you come round about midnight—"

"I'll be sure to," Eldred said eagerly. "I'm going to be in this thing. And I want to know all about that explosive idea."

II

Martin Hackness dressed with less than his usual care that evening. He even forgot that Miss Cynthia Grimfern had a strong prejudice in favour of black evening ties, and, usually, he paid a great deal of deference to her opinions. But he was thinking of other matters now. There was no sign of anything abnormal as Hackness drove along in the direction of Clarence Terrace. The night was more than typically yellow for the time of year, but there was no kind of trouble with the traffic, though down the river the fairway lay under a dense bank of cloud.

Hackness sniffed the air eagerly. He detected or thought he detected a certain acrid suggestion in the atmosphere. As the cab approached Trafalgar Square Hackness could hear shouts and voices raised high in protestation. Suddenly his cab seemed to be plunged into a wall of darkness.

It was so swift and unexpected that it came with the force of a blow. The horse appeared to have trotted into a bank of dense blackness. The wall had shut down so swiftly, blotting out a section of London, that Hackness could only gaze at it with mouth wide open.

Hackness hopped out of his cab hurriedly. So sheer and stark was the black wall that the horse was out of sight. Mechanically the driver reigned back. The horse came back to the cab with the dazzling swiftness of a conjuring trick. A thin stream of breeze wandered from the direction of Whitehall. It was this air finding its way up the funnel formed by the sheet that cut off the fog to a razor edge.

"Been teetotal for eighteen years," the cabman muttered, "so that's all right. And what do you please to make of it, sir?"

Hackness muttered something incoherent. As he stood there, the black wall lifted like a stage curtain, and he found himself under the lee of an omnibus. In a dazed kind of way he patted the cabhorse on the flank. He looked at his hand. It was greasy and oily and grimy as if he had been in the engine-room of a big liner.

"Get on as fast as you can," he cried. "It was fog, just a little present from the burning petroleum. Anyway, it's gone now."

True, the black curtain had lifted, but the atmosphere reeked with the odour of burning oil. The lamps and shop windows were splashed and mottled with something that might have passed for black snow. Traffic had been brought to a standstill for the moment, eager knots of pedestrians were discussing the situation with alarm and agitation, a man in evening dress was busily engaged in a vain attempt to remove sundry black patches from his shirt front.

Sir Edgar Grimfern was glad to see his young friend. Had Grimfern been comparatively poor, and less addicted to big game shooting, he would doubtless have proved a great scientific light. Anything with a dash of adventure fascinated him. He was enthusiastic on flying machines and aeroplanes generally. There were big workshops at the back of 119, Clarence Terrace, where Hackness put in a good deal of his spare time. Those two were going to startle the world presently.

Hackness shook hands thoughtfully with Cynthia Grimfern. There was a slight frown on her pretty intellectual face as she noted his tie.

"There's a large smut on it," she remarked, "and it serves you right."

Hackness explained. He had a flattering audience. He told of the strange happening in Trafalgar Square and the majestic scene on the river. He gave a graphic account of the theory that he had built upon it. There was an animated discussion all through dinner.

"The moral of which is that we are going to be plunged into Cimmerian darkness," Cynthia said, "that is, if the fog comes down. If you think you are going to frighten me out of my evening's entertainment you are mistaken."

All the same it had grown much darker and thicker as the trio drove off in the direction of the Lyceum Theatre. There were patches of dark acrid fog here and there like ropes of smoke into which figures passed and disappeared only to come out on the other side choking and coughing. So local were these swathes of fog that in a wide thoroughfare it was possible to partially avoid them. Festoons of vapour hung from one lampost to another, the air was filled with a fatty sickening odour.

"How nasty," Cynthia exclaimed. "Mr. Hackness, please close that window. I am almost sorry that we started. What's that?"

There was a shuffling movement under the seat of the carriage, the quick bark of a dog; Cynthia's little fox terrier had stolen into the brougham. It was a favourite trick of his, the girl explained.

"He'll go back again," she said. "Kim knows that he has done wrong."

That Kim was forgotten and discovered later on coiled up under the stall of his mistress was a mere detail. Hackness was too preoccupied to feel any uneasiness. He was only conscious that the electric lights were growing dim and yellow, and that a brown haze was coming between the auditorium and the stage. When the curtain fell on the third act it was hardly possible to see across the theatre. Two or three large heavy blots of some greasy matter fell on to the white shoulders of a lady in the stalls to be hastily wiped away by her companion. They left a long greasy smear behind.

"I can hardly breathe," Cynthia gasped. "I wish I had stopped at home. Surely those electric lights are going out."

But the lights were merely being wrapped in a filament that every moment grew more and more dense. As the curtain went up again there was just the suspicion of a draught from the back of the stage, and the whole of it was smothered in a small brown cloud that left absolutely nothing to the view. It was impossible now to make out a single word of the programme, even when it was held close to the eyes.

"Hackness was right," Grimfern growled. "We had far better have stayed at home."

Hackness said nothing. He had no pride in the accuracy of his forecast. Perhaps he was the only man in London who knew what the full force of this catastrophe meant. It grew so dark now that he could see no more than the mere faint suggestion of his fair companion, something was falling out of the gloom like black ragged snow. As the pall lifted just for an instant he could see the dainty dresses of the women absolutely smothered with the thick oily smuts. The reek of petroleum was stifling.

There was a frightened scream from behind, and a yell out of the ebony wall to the effect that somebody had fainted. Someone was speaking from the stage with a view to stay what might prove to be a dangerous panic. Another sombre wave filled the theatre and then it grew absolutely black, so black that a match held a foot or so from the nose could not be seen. One of the plagues of Egypt with all its horrors had fallen upon London.

"Let us try and make our way out," Hackness suggested. "Go quietly."

Others seemed to be moved by the same idea. It was too black and dark for anything like a rush, so that a dangerous panic was out of the question. Slowly but surely the fashionable audience reached the vestibule, the hall, and the steps.

Nothing to be seen, no glimmer of anything, no sound of traffic. The destroying angel might have passed over London and blotted out all human life. The magnitude of the disaster had frightened London's millions as it fell.

III

A city of the blind! Six millions of people suddenly deprived of sight! The disaster sounds impossible—a nightmare, the wild vapourings of a diseased imagination—and yet why not? Given a favourable atmospheric condition, something colossal in the way of a fire, and there it is. And there, somewhere folded away in the book of Nature, is the simple remedy.

Such thoughts as these flashed through Hackness's mind as he stood under the portico of the Lyceum Theatre, quite helpless and inert for the moment.

But the darkness was thicker and blacker than anything he had ever imagined. It was absolutely the darkness that could be felt. Hackness could hear the faint scratching of matches all around him, but there was no glimmer of light anywhere. And the atmosphere was thick, stifling, greasy. Yet it was not quite as stifling as perfervid imagination suggested. The very darkness suggested suffocation. Still, there was air, a sultry light breeze that set the murk in motion, and mercifully brought from some purer area the oxygen that made life possible. There was always air, thank God, to the end of the Four Days' Night.

Nobody spoke for a time. Not a sound of any kind could be heard. It was odd to think that a few miles away the country might be sleeping under the clear stars. It was terrible to think that hundreds of thousands of people must be standing lost in the streets and yet near to home.

A little way off a dog whined, a child in a sweet refined voice cried that she was lost. An anxious mother called in reply. The little one had been forgotten in the first flood of that awful darkness. By sheer good luck Hackness was enabled to locate the child. He could feel that her wraps were rich and costly, though the same fatty slime was upon them. He caught the child up in his arms and yelled that he had got her. The mother was close by, yet full five minutes elapsed before Hackness blundered upon her. Something was whining and fawning about his feet.

He called upon Grimfern, and the latter answered in his ear. Cynthia was crying pitifully and helplessly. Some women there were past that.

"For Heaven's sake tell us what we are to do," Grimfern gasped. "I flatter myself that I know London well, but I couldn't find my way home in this."

Something was licking Hackness's hand. It was the dog Kim. There was just a chance here. He tore his handkerchief in strips and knotted it together. One end he fastened to the little dog's collar.

"It's Kim," he explained. "Tell the dog 'home.' There's just a chance that he may lead you home. We're very wonderful creatures, but one sensible dog is worth a million of us to-night. Try it."

"And where are you going?" Cynthia asked. She spoke high, for a babel of voices had broken out. "What will become of you?"

"Oh, I am all right," Hackness said with an affected cheerfulness. "You see, I was fairly sure that this would happen sooner or later. So I pigeon-holed a way of dealing with the difficulty. Scotland Yard listened, but thought me a bore all the same. This is the situation where I come in."

Grimfern touched the dog and urged him forward.

Kim gave a little bark and a whine. His muscular little body strained at the leash.

"It's all right," Grimfern cried. "Kim understands. That queer little pill-box of a brain of his is worth the finest intellect in England to-night."

Cynthia whispered a faint good-night, and Hackness was alone. As he stood there in the blackness the sense of suffocation was overwhelming. He essayed to smoke a cigarette, but he hadn't the remotest idea whether the thing was alight or not. It had no taste or flavour.

But it was idle to stand there. He must fight his way along to Scotland Yard to persuade the authorities to listen to his ideas. There was not the slightest danger of belated traffic, no sane man would have driven a horse in such dense night. Hackness blundered along without the faintest idea to which point of the compass he was facing.

If he could only get his bearings he felt that he should be all right. He found his way into the Strand at length; he fumbled up against someone and asked where he was. A hoarse voice responded that the owner fancied it was somewhere in Piccadilly.

There were scores of people in the streets standing about talking desperately, absolute strangers clinging to one another for sheer craving for company to keep the frayed senses together. The most fastidious clubman there would have chummed with the toughest Hooligan rather than have his own thoughts for company.

Hackness pushed his way along. If he got out of his bearings he adopted the simple experiment of knocking at the first door he came to and asking where he was. His reception was not invariably enthusiastic, but it was no time for nice distinctions. And a deadly fear bore everybody down.

At last he came to Scotland Yard, as the clocks proclaimed that it was half-past one. Ghostly official voices told Hackness the way to Inspector Williamson's office, stern officials grasped him by the arm and piloted him up flights of stairs. He blundered over a chair and sat down. Out of the black cavern of space Inspector Williamson spoke.

"I am thankful you have come. You are just the man I most wanted to see. I want my memory refreshed over that scheme of yours," he said. "I didn't pay very much attention to it at the time."

"Of course you didn't. Did you ever know an original prophet who wasn't laughed at? Still, I don't mind confessing that I hardly anticipated anything quite so awful as this. The very density of it makes some parts of my scheme impossible. We shall have to shut our teeth and endure it. Nothing really practical can be done so long as this fog lasts."

"But, man alive, how long will it last?"

"Perhaps an hour or perhaps a week. Do you grasp what an awful calamity faces us?"

Williamson had no reply. So long as the fog lasted, London was in a state of siege, and, not only this, but every house in it was a fort, each depending upon itself for supplies. No bread could be baked, no meal could be carried round, no milk or vegetables delivered so long as the fog remained. Given a day or two of this and thousands of families would be on the verge of starvation. It was not a pretty picture that Hackness drew, but Williamson was bound to agree with every word of it.

These two men sat in the darkness till what should have been the dawn, whilst scores of subordinates were setting some sort of machinery in motion to preserve order.

Hackness stumbled home to his rooms about nine o'clock in the morning, without having succeeded in persuading the officials to grant him permission to experiment. Mechanically he felt for his watch to see the time. The watch was gone. Hackness smiled grimly. The predatory classes had not been quite blind to the advantages of the situation.

There was no breakfast for Hackness for the simple reason that it had been found impossible to light the kitchen fire. But there was a loaf of bread, some cheese, and a knife. Hackness fumbled for his bottled beer and a glass. There were many worse breakfasts in London that morning.

He woke presently, conscious that a clock was striking nine. After some elaborate thought and the asking of a question or two from another inmate of the house, Hackness found to his horror that he had slept the clock round nearly twice. It was nine o'clock in the morning, twenty-three hours since he had fallen asleep! And, so far as Hackness could judge, there were no signs of the fog's abatement.

He changed his clothes and washed the greasy slime off him so far as cold water and soap would allow. There were plenty of people in the streets, hunting for food for the most part; there were tales of people found dead in the gutters. Progression was slow but the utter absence of traffic rendered it safe and possible. Men spoke with bated breath, the weight of the great calamity upon them.

News that came from a few miles outside the radius spoke of clear skies and bright sunshine. There was a great deal of sickness, and the doctors had more than they could manage, especially with the young and the delicate.

And the calamity looked like getting worse. Six million people were breathing what oxygen there was. Hackness returned to his chambers to find Eldred awaiting him.

"This can't go on, you know," the latter said tersely.

"Of course it can't," Hackness replied. "All the air is getting exhausted. Come with me down to Scotland Yard and help to try and persuade Williamson to test my experiment."

"What! Do you mean to say he is still obstinate?"

"Well, perhaps he feels different to-day. Come along."

Williamson was in a chastened frame of mind. He had no optimistic words when Hackness suggested that nothing less than a violent meteorological disturbance would clear the deadly peril of the fog away. It was time for drastic remedies, and if they failed things would be no worse than before.

"But can you manage it?" Williamson asked.

"I fancy so," Hackness replied. "It's a risk, of course, but everything has been ready for a long time. We could start after tomorrow midnight, or any time for that matter."

"Very well," Williamson sighed with the air of a man who realises that after all the tooth must come out. "If this produces a calamity I shall be asked to send in my resignation. If I refuse—"

"If you refuse there is more than a chance that you won't want another situation," Hackness said grimly. "Let's get the thing going, Eldred."

They crawled along through the black suffocating darkness, feeble, languid, and sweating at every pore. There was a murky closeness in the vitiated atmosphere that seemed to take all the strength and energy away. At any other time the walk to Clarence Terrace would have been a pleasure, now it was a penance. They found their objective after a deal of patience and trouble. Hackness yelled in the doorway. There was a sound of footsteps and Cynthia Grimfern spoke.

"Ah, what a relief it is to know that you are all right," she said. "I pictured all sorts of horrors happening to you. Will this never end, Martin?"

She cried softly in her distress. Hackness felt for her hand and pressed it tenderly.

"We are going to try my great theory," he said. "Eldred is with me, and we have got Williamson's permission to operate with the aeroplane. Where is Sir Edgar?"

Grimfern was in the big workshop in the garden. As best he could, he was fumbling over some machinery for the increase of power in electric lighting. Hackness took a queer-looking lamp with double reflectors from his pocket.

"Shut off that dynamo," he said, "and give me the flex. I've got a little idea here Bramley, the electrician, lent me. With that 1000-volt generator of yours I can get a light equal to 40,000 candles. There."

Flick went the switch, and the others staggered back with their hands to their eyes. The great volume of light, impossible to face under ordinary circumstances, illuminated the workshop with a faint glow like a winter's dawn. It was sufficient for all practical purpose, but to eyes that had seen absolutely nothing for two days and nights very painful.

Cynthia laughed hysterically. She saw the men grimed and dirty, blackened and greasy, as if they were fresh from a stoker's hole in a tropical sea. They saw a tall, graceful girl in the droll parody of a kitchen-maid who had wiped a tearful face with a blacklead brush.

But they could see. Along the whole floor of the workshop lay a queer, cigar-shaped instrument with grotesque wings and a tail like that of a fish, but capable of being turned in any direction. It seemed a problem to get this strange-looking monster out of the place, but as the whole of the end of the workshop was constructed to pull out, the difficulty was not great.

This was Sir Edgar Grimfern's aeroplane, built under his own eyes and with the assistance of Hackness and Eldred.

"It will be a bit of risk in the dark," Sir Edgar said thoughtfully.

"It will, sir, but I hope it will mean the saving of a great city," Hackness remarked. "We shall have no difficulty in getting up, and as to the getting down, don't forget that the atmosphere a few miles beyond the outskirts of London is quite clear. If only the explosives are strong enough!"

"Don't theorise," Eldred snapped. "We've got a good day's work before we start. And there is no time to be lost."

"Luncheon first," Sir Edgar suggested "served in here. It will be plain and cold; but, thank goodness, there is plenty of it. My word, after that awful darkness what a blessed thing light is once more!"

Two hours after midnight the doors of the workshop were pulled away and the aeroplane was dragged on its carriage into the garden. The faint glimmer of light only served to make the blackness all the thicker. The three men waved their hands silently to Cynthia and jumped in. A few seconds later and they were whirred and screwed away into the suffocating fog.

IV

London was holding out doggedly and stolidly. Scores of houses watched and waited for missing ones who would never return, the streets and the river had taken their toll, in open spaces, in the parks, and on the heaths many were shrouded. But the long black night held its secret well. There had been some ruffianism and plundering at first. But what was the use of plunder to the thief who could not dispose of his booty, who could not exchange a rare diamond for so much as a mouthful of bread? Some of them could not even find their way home, they had to remain in the streets where there was the dread of the lifting blanket and the certainty of punishment with the coming of the day.

But if certain houses mourned the loss of inmates, some had more than their share. Belated women, frightened business girls, caught in the fog had sought the first haven at hand, and there they were free to remain. There were sempstresses in Mayfair, and delicately-nurtured ladies in obscure Bloomsbury boarding-houses. Class distinction seemed to be remote as the middle ages.

Scotland Yard, the local authorities, and the County Council had worked splendidly together. Provisions were short, though a good deal of bread and milk had with greatest difficulty been imported from outside the radius of the scourge. Still the poor were suffering acutely, and the cries of frightened children were heard in every street. A few days more and the stoutest nerves must give way. Nobody could face such a blackness and retain their senses for long. London was a city of the blind. Sleep was the only panacea for the creeping madness.

There were few deeds of violence done. The most courageous, the most bloodthirsty man grew mild and gentle before the scourge. Desperate men prowled about in search of food, but they wanted nothing else. Certainly they would not have attempted violence to get it.

Alarmists predicted that in a few hours life in London would be impossible. For once they had reason on their side. Every hour the air, or what passed for air, grew more poisonous. Men fancied a city with six million corpses!

The calamity would kill big cities altogether. No great mass of people would ever dare to congregate together again where manufacturers made a hideous atmosphere overhead. It would be a great check upon the race for gold. There was much justification for this morbid condition of public feeling.

So the third long weary day dragged to an end, and people went to bed in the old mechanical fashion hoping for better signs in the morning. How many weary years since they had last seen the sunshine, colour, anything?

There was a change from the black monotony some time after dawn. Most people had nearly lost all sense of time when dawn ought to have been. People were struggling back to their senses again, trying to pierce the thick curtain that held everything in bondage. Doors were opened and restless ones passed into the street.

Suddenly there was a smiting shock from somewhere, a deafening splitting roar in the ears, and central London shivered. It was as if some mighty explosion had taken place in space, and as if the same concussion had been followed by a severe shock of earthquake.

Huge buildings shook and trembled, furniture was overturned, and from every house came the smash of glass. Was this merely a fog or some thick curtain that veiled the approaching dissolution of the world? People stood still, trembling and wondering. And before the question was answered, a strange thing, a modern miracle happened. A great arc of the blackness peeled off and stripped the daylight bare before their startled eyes.

V

The work was full of a real live peril, but the aeroplane was cast loose at length. Its upward motion was slow, perhaps owing to the denseness of the atmosphere. For some time nobody spoke. Something seemed to oppress their breathing. They were barely conscious of the faint upward motion. If they only rose perfectly straight all would be well.

"That's a fine light you had in the workshop," said Eldred. "But why not have established a few hundreds of them—"

"All over London," Hackness cut in, "For the simple reason that the lamp my friend lent me is the only one in existence. It is worked at a dangerous voltage too."

The upward motion continued. The sails of the aeroplane rustled slightly. Grimfern drew a deep breath.

"Air," he gasped, "real pure fresh air! Do you notice it?"

The cool sweetness of it filled their lungs. The sudden effect was almost intoxicating. A wild desire to laugh and shout and sing came over them. Then gradually three human faces and a ghostly shaped aeroplane emerged out of nothingness. They could see one another plainly now; they felt the upward rush; they were passing through a misty envelope that twisted and curled like live ropes. Another minute and they were beyond the fog belt.

They looked at one another and laughed. All three of them were blackened and grimed and greasy, smothered from head to foot in fatty soot flakes. Three more disreputable looking ruffians it would have been hard to imagine. There was something grotesque in the reflection that every Londoner was the same.

It was light now, broad daylight, with a round globe of sun climbing up out of the pearly mists in the East. They revelled in the brightness and the light. Below them lay the thick layers of fog that would be a shroud in earnest if nothing came to dispel it.

"We're a thousand feet above the city," Eldred said presently. "We had better pay out five hundred feet of cable."

To a hook at the end of a flexible wire Hackness attached a large bomb filled with a certain high explosive. Through the eye of the hook another wire—an electric one—was attached. The whole thing was carefully lowered to the full extent of the cable. Two anxious faces peered from the car. Grimfern appeared to be playing carelessly with a polished switch spliced into the wire. But his hands were shaking.

Eldred nodded. He had no words to spare just then.

Grimfern's forefinger pressed the polished button, there was a snap and almost immediately a roar and a rush of air that set the aeroplane rocking violently. All about them the clouds were spinning, below the foggy envelope was twisted and torn as smoke is blown away from a huge stack by a high wind.

"Look," Hackness yelled. "Look at that!"

He pointed downwards. The force of the explosion had literally torn a hole in the dense foggy curtain. The brilliant light of day shone through down into London as from a gigantic skylight.

This is what the amazed inhabitants of central London saw as they rushed out of their houses after what they imagined to be a shock of earthquake. The effect was weird, wonderful, one never to be forgotten. From a radius of half a mile from St. Paul's, London was flooded with brilliant light. People rubbed their eyes, unable to face the sudden and blinding glare. They gasped and thrilled with exultation as a column of fresh sweet air rushed to fill the vacuum. As yet they knew nothing of the cause.

That brilliant shaft of light showed strange things. Every pavement was black as ink, the fronts of the houses looked as if they had been daubed over with pitch. The roads were dark with fatty soot. On Ludgate Hill were dozens of vehicles from which the horses had been detached. There were numerous motor cars apparently lacking owners. A pickpocket sat in the gutter with a pile of costly trinkets about him, gems that glittered in the mud. These things had been collected before the fog grew beyond endurance. Now they were about as useful to the thief as an elephant might have been.

At the end of five minutes the curtain fell again. The flying, panic- stricken pickpocket huddled down once more with a frightened curse.

But London was no longer alarmed. A passing glimpse of the aeroplane had been seen, and better informed folks knew what was taking place. Presently another explosion followed, tearing the curtain away over Hampstead; for the next two hours the explosions continued at short intervals. There were tremendous outbursts of cheering whenever the relief came.

Presently a little light seemed to be coming. Ever and again it was possible for a man to see his hands before his face. Above the fog banks a wrack of cloud had gathered, the aeroplane was coated with a glittering mist. An hour before it had been perfectly fair overhead. Then it began to rain in earnest. The constant explosions had summoned up and brought down the rain as the heavy discharge of artillery used to do in the days of the Boer War.

It came down in a drenching stream that wetted the occupants of the aeroplane to the skin. They did not seem to mind. The exhilaration of the fresh sweet air was still in their veins, they worked on at their bombs till the last ounce of the high explosives was exhausted.

The rain was seen to fall...
And the rain was falling over London. Wherever a hole was torn in the curtain, the rain was seen to fall—black rain as thick as ink and quite as disfiguring. The whole city wore a suit of mourning.

"The cloud is passing away," Eldred cried. "I can see the top of St. Paul's."

Surely enough, the cross seemed to lift skyward. Bit by bit and inch by inch the panorama of London slowly unfolded itself. Despite the sooty flood—a flood gradually growing cleaner and sweeter every moment—the streets were filled with people gazing up in fascination at the aeroplane.

The tumult of their cheers came upwards. It was their thanks for the forethought and scientific knowledge that had proved to be the salvation of London. As a matter of fact, the high explosives had only been the indirect means of preserving countless lives. The conjuring up of that heavy rain had been the real salvation. It had condensed the fog and beaten it down to earth in a sooty flow of water. It was a heavy, sloppy, gloomy day, such as London ever enjoys the privilege of grumbling over, but nobody grumbled now. The blessed daylight had come back, it was possible to fill the lungs with something like pure air once more, and to realise the simple delight of living.

Nobody minded the rain, nobody cared an atom for the knowledge that he was a little worse and a little more grimy than the dirtiest sweep alive. What did it matter so long as everybody was alike? Looking down, the trio in the aeroplane could see London grow mad, grave men skipping about in the rain like schoolboys at the first fall of snow.

"We had better get down," said Grimfern. "Otherwise we shall have an ovation ready for us, and, personally, I should prefer a breakfast. In a calm like this we need not have any difficulty in making Regent's Park safely."

The valve was opened and the great car dropped like a flashing bird. They saw the rush in the streets, they could hear the tramp of feet now. They dropped at length in what looked like a yelling crowd of demented Hottentots.

VI

The aeroplane was safely housed once more, the yelling mob had departed. London was bent upon one of its occasional insane holidays. The pouring rain did not matter one jot—had not the rain proved to be the salvation of the great city? What did it matter that the streets were black and the people blacker still? The danger was averted. "We will go out and explore presently," said Grimfern. "Meanwhile, breakfast. A thing like this must never occur again, Hackness." Hackness sincerely hoped not. Cynthia Grimfern came out to meet them. A liberal application of soap and water had rendered her sweet and fair, but it was impossible to keep clean for long. Everywhere lay evidences of the fog.

"It's lovely to be able to see and breathe once more," she said. "Last night every moment I felt as if I must be suffocated. To-day it is like suddenly finding Paradise."

"A sooty paradise," Grimfern growled.

Cynthia laughed a little hopelessly.

"It's dreadful," she said. "I have had no table-cloth laid, it is useless. But the table itself is clean, and that is something. I don't think London will ever be perfectly clean again."

The reek was still upon the great city, the taint of it hung upon the air. By one o'clock it had ceased raining and the sky cleared A startled sun looked down on strange things. There was a curious thickness about the trees in Regent's Park, they were as black as if they had been painted. The pavements were greasy and dangerous to pedestrians in a hurry.

There was a certain jubilation still to be observed, but the black melancholy desolation was bound to depress the most exuberant spirits. For the last three days everything had been at a standstill.

In the thickly populated districts the mortality amongst little children had been alarmingly high. Those who had any tendency to lung or throat or chest troubles died like flies before the first breath of frost. The evening papers, coming out as usual, a little late in the day, had many a gruesome story to tell. It was the harvest of the scare-line journalist, and he lost no chance. He scented his gloomy copy and tracked it down unerringly.

Over two thousand children—to say nothing of elderly people—had died in the East End. The very small infants had had no chance at all.

The Lord Mayor promptly started a Mansion House fund. There would be work and to spare presently. Meanwhile tons upon tons of machinery stood idle until it could be cleaned; all the trade of London was disorganised.

The river and the docks had taken a dreadful toll. Scores of labourers and sailors overtaken by the sudden scourge, had blundered into the water to be seen no more. The cutting off of the railways and other communications that brought London its daily bread had produced a temporary, but no less painful lack of provisions.

"It's a lamentable state of things," Grimfern said moodily as the two trudged back to Regent's Park later in the evening. It was impossible to get a cab for the simple reason that there was not one in London fit to be used. "But I don't see how we are going to better it. We can dispel the fogs, but not before they have done terrible damage."

"There is an easy way out of the difficulty," Eldred said quietly.

The others turned eagerly to listen. As a rule Eldred did not speak until he had thought the matter deliberately out.

"Abolish all fires throughout the Metropolitan area," he said. "In time it will have to be done. All London must warm itself and cook its food and drive all its machinery by electric power. Then it will be one of the healthiest towns in the universe. Everything done by electric power. No thousands of chimneys belching forth black poisonous smoke, but a clear, pure atmosphere. In towns like Brighton, where the local authorities have grappled the question in earnest, electric power is half the cost of gas.

"If only London combined it would be less than that. No dirt, no dust, no smell, no smoke! The magnificent system at Brighton never cost the ratepayers anything, indeed a deal of the profit has gone to the relief of the local burdens. Perhaps this dire calamity will rouse London to a sense of its dangers—but I doubt it."

Eldred shook his head despondingly at the dark chaos of the park. Perhaps he was thinking of the victims that the disaster had claimed. The others had followed sadly, and Grimfern, leading the way into his house banged the door on the darkening night.

THE DUST OF DEATH

The front door bell tinkled impatiently; evidently somebody was in a hurry. Alan Hubert answered the call, a thing that even a distinguished physician might do, seeing that it was on the stroke of midnight. The tall, graceful figure of a woman in evening dress stumbled into the hall. The diamonds in her hair shimmered and trembled, her face was full of terror.

"You are Dr. Hubert," she gasped. "I am Mrs. Fillingham, the artist's wife, you know. Will you come with me at once... My husband... I had been dining out. In the studio... Oh, please come!"

Hubert asked no unnecessary questions. He knew Fillingham, the great portrait painter, well enough by repute and by sight also, for Fillingham's house and studio were close by. There were many artists in the Devonshire Park district—that pretty suburb which was one of the triumphs of the builder's and landscape gardener's art. Ten years ago it had been no more than a swamp; to-day people spoke complacently of the fact that they lived in Devonshire Park.

Hubert walked up the drive and past the trim lawns with Mrs. Fillingham hanging on his arm, and in at the front door. Mrs. Fillingham pointed to a door on the right. She as too exhausted to speak. There were shaded lights gleaming everywhere, on old oak and armour and on a large portrait of a military-looking man propped up on an easel. On a lay figure was a magnificent foreign military uniform.

Hubert caught all this in a quick mental flash. But the vital interest to him was a human figure lying on his back before the fireplace. The clean-shaven, sensitive face of the artist had a ghastly, purple-black tinge, there was a large swelling in the throat.

"He—he is not dead?" Mrs. Fillingham asked in a frozen whisper.

Hubert was able to satisfy the distracted wife on that head. Fillingham was still breathing. Hubert stripped the shade from a reading lamp and held the electric bulb at the end of its long flex above the sufferer's mouth, contriving to throw the flood of light upon the back of the throat.

'Diphtheria!' he exclaimed.
"Diphtheria!" he exclaimed. "Label's type unless I am greatly mistaken. Some authorities are disposed to scoff at Dr. Label's discovery. I was an assistant of his for four years and I know better. Fortunately I happen to know what the treatment—successful in two cases—was."

He hurried from the house and returned a few minutes later breathlessly. He had some strange-looking, needle-like instruments in his hands. He took an electric lamp from its socket and substituted a plug on a flex instead. Then he cleared a table without ceremony and managed to hoist his patient upon it.

"Now please hold that lamp steadily thus," he said. "Bravo, you are a born nurse! I am going to apply these electric needles to the throat."

Hubert talked on more for the sake of his companion's nerves than anything else. The still figure on the table quivered under his touch, his lungs expanded in a long, shuddering sigh. The heart was beating more or less regularly now. Fillingham opened his eyes and muttered something.

"Ice," Hubert snapped, "have you got any ice in the house?"

It was a well-regulated establishment and there was plenty of ice in the refrigerator. Not until the patient was safe in bed did Hubert's features relax.

"We'll pull him through yet," he said. "I'll send you a competent nurse round in half-an-hour. I'll call first thing in the morning and bring Dr. Label with me. He must not miss this on any account."

Half-an-hour later Hubert was spinning along in a hansom towards Harley Street. It was past one when he reached the house of the great German savant. A dim light was burning in the hall. A big man with an enormous shaggy head and a huge frame attired in the seediest of dress coats welcomed Hubert with a smile.

"So, my young friend," Label said, "your face promises excitement."

"Case of Label's diphtheria," Hubert said crisply. "Fillingham, the artist, who lives close by me. Fortunately they called me in. I have arranged for you to see my patient the first thing in the morning."

The big German's jocular manner vanished. He led Hubert gravely to a chair in his consulting-room and curtly demanded details. He smiled approvingly as Hubert enlarged upon his treatment of the case.

"Undoubtedly your diagnosis was correct," he said, puffing furiously at a long china pipe. "You have not forgotten what I told you of it. The swelling—which is caused by violent blood poisoning—yielded to the electric treatment. I took the virus from the cases in the north and I tried them on scores of animals. And they all died.

"I find it is the virus of what is practically a new disease, one of the worst in the wide world. I say it recurs again, and it does. So I practise, and practise to find a cure. And electricity is the cure. I inoculate five dogs with the virus and I save two by the electric current. You follow my plans and you go the first stage of the way to cure Fillingham. Did you bring any of that mucous here?"

Hubert produced it in a tiny glass tube. For a little time Label examined it under his microscope. He wanted to make assurance doubly sure.

"It is the same thing," he said presently. "I knew that it was bound to recur again. Why, it is planted all over our big cities. And electricity is the only way to get rid of it. It was the best method of dealing with sewage, only corporations found it too expensive. Wires in the earth charged to say 10,000 volts. Apply this and you destroy the virus that lies buried under hundreds of houses in London. They laughed at me when I suggested it years ago."

"Underground," Hubert asked vaguely.

"Ach, underground, yes. Don't you recollect that in certain parts of England cancer is more common than in other places? The germs have been turned up in fields. I, myself, have proved their existence. In a little time, perhaps. I shall open the eyes of your complacent Londoners. You live in a paradise, ach Gott! And what was that paradise like ten years ago? Dreary pools and deserted brickfields. And how do you fill it up and level it to build houses upon?"

"By the carting of hundreds of thousands of loads of refuse, of course."

"Ach, I will presently show you what that refuse was and is. Now go home to bed."

Mrs. Fillingham remained in the studio with Hubert whilst Label was making his examination overhead. The patient had had a bad night; his symptoms were very grave indeed. Hubert listened more or less vaguely; his mind had gone beyond the solitary case. He was dreading what might happen in the future.

"Your husband has a fine constitution," he said soothingly.

"He has overtried it lately," Mrs. Fillingham replied. "At present he is painting a portrait of the Emperor of Asturia. His Majesty was to have sat to-day; he spent the morning here yesterday."

But Hubert was paying no attention.

The heavy tread of Label was heard as he floundered down the stairs. His big voice was booming. What mattered all the portraits in the world so long as the verdict hung on the German doctor's lips!

"Oh, there is a chance," Label exclaimed. "Just a chance. Everything possible is being done. This is not so much diphtheria as a new disease. Diphtheria family, no doubt, but the blood poisoning makes a difficult thing of it."

Label presently dragged Hubert away after parting with Mrs. Fillingham. He wanted to find a spot where building or draining was going on.

They found some men presently engaged in connecting a new house with the main drainage—a deep cutting some forty yards long by seven or eight feet deep. There was the usual crust of asphalt on the road, followed by broken bricks and the like, and a more or less regular stratum of blue-black rubbish, soft, wet, and clinging, and emitting an odour that caused Hubert to throw up his head.

"You must have broken into a drain somewhere here," he said.

"We ain't, sir," the foreman of the gang replied. "It's nout but rubbidge as they made up the road with here ten years ago. Lord knows where it came from, but it do smell fearful in weather like this."

The odour indeed was stifling. All imaginable kinds of rubbish and refuse lay under the external beauties of Devonshire Park in strata ranging from five to forty feet deep. It was little wonder that trees and flowers flourished here. And here—wet, and dark, and festering— was a veritable hotbed of disease. Contaminated rags, torn paper, road siftings, decayed vegetable matter, diseased food, fish and bones all were represented here.

"Every ounce of this ought to have gone through the destructor," Label snorted. "But no, it is used for the foundations of a suburban paradise. My word, we shall see what your paradise will be like presently. Come along."

Label picked up a square slab of the blue stratum, put it in a tin, and the tin in his pocket. He was snorting and puffing with contempt.

"Now come to Harley Street with me and I will show you things," he said.

He was as good as his word. Placed under a microscope, a minute portion of the subsoil from Devonshire Park proved to be a mass of living matter. There were at least four kinds of bacillus here that Hubert had never seen before. With his superior knowledge Label pointed out the fact that they all existed in the mucous taken from Fillingham on the previous evening.

"There you are!" He cried excitedly. "You get all that wet sodden refuse of London and you dump it down here in a heap. You mix with it a heap of vegetable matter so that fermentation shall have every chance. Then you cover it over with some soil, and you let it boil, boil, boil. Then, when millions upon millions of death-dealing microbes are bred and bred till their virility is beyond the scope of science, you build good houses on the top of it. For years I have been prophesying an outbreak of some new disease—or some awful form of an old one—and here it comes. They called me a crank because I asked for high electric voltage to kill the plague—to destroy it by lightning. A couple of high tension wires run into the earth and there you are. See here."

He took his cube of the reeking earth and applied the battery to it. The mass showed no outward change. But once under the microscope a fragment of it demonstrated that there was not the slightest trace of organic life.

"There!" Label cried. "Behold the remedy. I don't claim that it will cure in every case, because we hardly touch the diphtheretic side of the trouble. When there has been a large loss of life we shall learn the perfect remedy by experience. But this thing is coming, and your London is going to get a pretty bad scare. You have laid it down like port wine, and now that the thing is ripe you are going to suffer from the consequence. I have written articles in the Lancet, I have warned people, but they take not the slightest heed."

Hubert went back home thoughtfully. He found the nurse who had Fillingham's case in hand waiting for him in his consulting-room.

"I am just back from my walk," she said. "I wish you would call at Dr. Walker's at Elm Crescent. He has two cases exactly like Mr. Fillingham's, and he is utterly puzzled."

Hubert snatched his hat and his electric needles, and hurried away at once. He found his colleague impatiently waiting for him There were two children this time in one of the best appointed houses in Devonshire Park, suffering precisely as Fillingham had done. In each instance the electric treatment gave the desired result. Hubert hastily explained the whole matter to Walker.

"It's an awful business," the latter said, "Personally, I have a great respect for Label, and I feel convinced that he is right. If this thing spreads, property in Devonshire Park won't be worth the price of slum lodgings." By mid-day nineteen cases of the so-called diphtheria had been notified within the three miles area known as Devonshire Park. Evidently some recent excavations had liberated the deadly microbe. But there was no scare as yet. Label came down again hotfoot with as many assistants as he could get, and took up his quarters with Hubert. They were going to have a busy time.

It was after two before Hubert managed to run across to Fillingham's again. He stood in the studio waiting for Mrs. Fillingham. His mind was preoccupied and uneasy, yet he seemed to miss something from the studio. It was strange, considering that he had only been in the room twice before.

"Are you looking for anything?" Mrs. Fillingham asked.

"I don't know," Hubert exclaimed. "I seem to miss something. I've got it—the absence of the uniform."

"They sent for it," Mrs. Fillingham said vaguely. She was dazed for want of sleep. "The Emperor had to go to some function, and that was the only uniform of the kind he happened to have. He was to have gone away in it after his sitting to-day. My husband persuaded him to leave it when it was here yesterday, and—"

Hubert had cried out suddenly as if in pain.

"He was here yesterday—here, with your husband, and your husband with the diphtheria on him?"

Then the weary wife understood.

"Good heavens—"

But Hubert was already out of the room. He blundered on until he came to a hansom cab creeping along in the sunshine.

"Buckingham Palace," he gasped. "Drive like mad. A five-pound note for you if you get me there by three o'clock!"

Already Devonshire Park was beginning to be talked about. It was wonderful how the daily press got to the root of things. Hubert caught sight of more than one contents bill as he drove home that alluded to the strange epidemic.

Dr. Label joined Hubert presently in Mrs. Fillingham's home, rubbing his huge hands together. He knew nothing of the new dramatic developments. He asked where Hubert had been spending his time.

"Trying to save the life of your friend, the Emperor of Asturia," Hubert said. "He was here yesterday with Fillingham, and, though he seems well enough at present, he may have the disease on him now. What do you think of that?"

Hubert waited to see the great man stagger before the blow. Label smiled and nodded as he proceeded to light a cigarette.

"Good job too," he said. "I am honorary physician to the court of Asturia. I go back, there, as you know, when I finish my great work here. The Emperor I have brought through four or five illnesses, and if anything is wrong he always sends for me."

"But he might get the awful form of diphtheria!"

"Very likely," Label said coolly. "All these things are in the hands of Providence. I know that man's constitution to a hair, and if he gets the disease I shall pull him through for certain. I should like him to have it."

"In the name of all that is practical, why?"

"To startle the public," Label cried. He was mounted on his hobby now. He paced up and down the room in a whirl of tobacco smoke. "It would bring the matter home to everybody. Then perhaps something will be done. I preach and preach in vain. Only the Lancet backs me up at all. Many times I have asked for a quarter of a million of money, so that I can found a school for the electrical treatment of germ diseases. I want to destroy all malaria. All dirt in bulk, every bit of refuse that is likely to breed fever and the like, should be treated by electricity. I would take huge masses of deadly scourge and mountains of garbage, and render them innocent by the electric current. But no; that costs money, and your poverty-stricken Government cannot afford it. Given a current of 10,000 volts a year or two ago, and I could have rendered this one of the healthiest places in England. You only wanted to run those high voltage wires into the earth here and there, and behold the millions are slain, wiped out, gone for ever. Perhaps I will get it now."

London was beginning to get uneasy. There had been outbreaks before, but they were of the normal type. People, for instance, are not so frightened of smallpox as they used to be. Modern science has learnt to grapple with the fell disease and rob it of half its terrors. But this new and virulent form of diphtheria was another matter.

Hubert sat over his dinner that night, making mental calculations. There were nearly a thousand houses of varying sizes in Devonshire Park. Would it be necessary to abandon these? He took down a large scale map of London, and hastily marked in blue pencil those areas which had developed rapidly of recent years. In nearly all of these a vast amount of artificial ground had been necessary. Hubert was appalled as he calculated the number of jerry-built erections in these districts.

A servant came in and laid The Evening Wire upon the table. Hubert glanced at it. Nothing had been lost in the way of sensation. The story of the Emperor's visit to the district had been given great prominence. An inquiry at Buckingham Palace had elicited the fact that the story was true.

Well, perhaps no harm would come of it. Hubert finished a cigar and prepared to go out. As he flung the paper aside a paragraph in the stop press column—a solitary paragraph like an inky island in a sea of white—caught his eye.

"No alarm need be experienced as to the danger encountered by the Emperor of Asturia, but we are informed that His Majesty is prevented from dining at Marlborough House to-night owing to a slight cold and sore throat caught, it is stated, in the draughts at Charing Cross Station. The Emperor will go down to Cowes as arranged to-morrow."

Hubert shook his head doubtfully. The slight cold and sore throat were ominous. His mind dwelt upon the shadow of trouble as he made his way to the hospital. There had been two fresh cases during the evening and the medical staff were looking anxious and worried. They wanted assistance badly, and Hubert gave his to the full.

It was nearly eleven before Hubert staggered home. In the main business street of the suburb a news-shop was still open.

A flaming placard attracted the doctor's attention. It struck him like a blow.

"Alarming illness of the Asturian Emperor. His Majesty stricken down by the new disease. Latest bulletin from Buckingham Palace."

Almost mechanically Hubert bought a paper. There was not much beyond the curt information that the Emperor was dangerously ill.

Arrived home Hubert found a telegram awaiting him. He tore it open. The message was brief but to the point.

"Have been called in to Buckingham Palace, Label's diphtheria certain. Shall try and see you to-morrow morning. Label."

London was touched deeply and sincerely. A great sovereign had come over here in the most friendly fashion to show his good feeling for a kindred race. On the very start of a round of pleasure he had been stricken down like this.

The public knew all the details from the progress of that fateful uniform to the thrilling eight o'clock bulletin when the life of Rudolph III was declared to be in great danger. They knew that Dr. Label had been sent for post haste. The big German was no longer looked upon as a clever crank, but the one man who might be able to save London from a terrible scourge. And from lip to lip went the news that over two hundred cases of the new disease had now broken out in Devonshire Park.

People knew pretty well what it was and what was the cause now. Label's warning had come home with a force that nobody had expected. He had stolen away quite late for half-an-hour to his own house and there had been quite free with the pressmen. He extenuated nothing. The thing was bad, and it was going to be worse. So far as he could see, something of this kind w as inevitable. If Londoners were so blind as to build houses on teeming heaps of filth, why, London must be prepared to take the consequences.

Hubert knew nothing of this. He had fallen back utterly exhausted in his chair with the idea of taking a short rest—for nearly three hours he had been fast asleep. Somebody was shaking him roughly. He struggled back to the consciousness that Label was bending over him.

"Well, you are a nice fellow," the German grumbled.

"I was dead beat and worn out," Hubert said apologetically. "How is the Emperor?"

"His Majesty is doing as well as I can expect. It is a very bad case, however. I have left him in competent hands, so that I could run down here. They were asking for you at the hospital, presuming that you were busy somewhere. The place is full, and so arc four houses in the nearest terrace."

"Spreading like that?" Hubert exclaimed.

"Spreading like that! By this time tomorrow we shall have a thousand cases on our hands. The authorities are doing everything they can to help us, fresh doctors and nurses and stores are coming in all the time."

"You turn people out of their houses to make way then?"

Label smiled grimly. He laid his hand on Hubert's shoulder, and piloted him into the roadway. The place seemed to be alive with cabs and vehicles of all kinds. It was as if all the inhabitants of Devonshire Park were going away for their summer holidays simultaneously. The electric arcs shone down on white and frightened faces where joyous gaiety should have been. Here and there a child slept peacefully, but on the whole it was a sorry exodus.

"There you are," Label said grimly. "It is a night flight from the plague. It has been going on for hours. It would have been finished now but for the difficulty in getting conveyances. Most of the cabmen are avoiding the place as if it were accursed. But money can command everything, hence the scene that you see before you."

Hubert stood silently watching the procession. There was very little luggage on any of the cabs or conveyances. Families were going wholesale. Devonshire Park for the most part was an exceedingly prosperous district, so that the difficulties of emigration were not great. In their panic the people were abandoning everything in the wild flight for life and safety.

Then he went in again to rest before the unknown labours of to-morrow. Next morning he anxiously opened his morning paper.

It was not particularly pleasant reading beyond the information that the health of the Emperor of Asturia was mentioned, and that he had passed a satisfactory night. As to the rest, the plague was spreading. There were two hundred and fifty cases in Devonshire Park. Label's sayings had come true at last; it was a fearful vindication of his prophecy. And the worst of it was that no man could possibly say where it was going to end.

Strange as it may seem, London's anxiety as to the welfare of one man blinded all to the great common danger. For the moment Devonshire Park was forgotten. The one centre of vivid interest was Buckingham Palace.

For three days crowds collected there until at length Label and his colleagues were in a position to issue a bulletin that gave something more than hope. The Emperor of Asturia was going to recover. Label was not the kind of man to say so unless he was pretty sure of his ground.

It was not till this fact had soaked itself into the public mind that attention was fully turned to the danger that threatened London. Devonshire Park was practically in quarantine. All those who could get away had done so, and those who had remained were confined to their own particular district, and provisioned on a system. The new plague was spreading fast.

In more than one quarter the suggestion was made that all houses in certain localities should be destroyed, and the ground thoroughly cleansed and disinfected. It would mean a loss of millions of money, but in the scare of the moment London cared nothing for that.

At the end of a week there were seven thousand cases of the new form of diphtheria under treatment. Over one thousand cases a day came in. Devonshire Park was practically deserted save for the poorer quarters, whence the victims came. It seemed strange to see fine houses abandoned to the first comer who had the hardihood to enter. Devonshire Park was a stricken kingdom within itself, and the Commune of terror reigned.

Enterprising journalists penetrated the barred area and wrote articles about it. One of the fraternity bolder than the rest passed a day and night in one of these deserted palatial residences, and gave his sensations to the Press. Within a few hours most of the villas were inhabited again! There were scores of men and women in the slums who have not the slightest fear of disease—they are too familiar with it for that—and they came creeping westward in search of shelter. The smiling paradise had become a kind of Tom Tiddlers ground, a huge estate in Chancery.

Nobody had troubled, the tenants were busy finding pure quarters elsewhere, the owners of the property were fighting public opinion to save what in many cases was their sole source of income. If Devonshire Park had to be razed to the ground many a wealthy man would be ruined.

It was nearly the end of the first week before this abnormal state of affairs was fully brought home to Hubert. He had been harassed and worried and worn by want of sleep, but tired as he was he did not fail to notice the number of poorer patients who dribbled regularly into the terrace of houses that now formed the hospital. There was something about them that suggested any district rather than Devonshire Park.

"What does it mean, Walker?" he asked one of his doctors.

Walker had just come in from his hour's exercise, heated and excited.

"It's a perfect scandal," he cried. "The police are fighting shy of us altogether. I've just been up to the station and they tell me it is a difficult matter to keep competent of officers in the district. All along Frinton Hill and Eversley Gardens the houses are crowded with outcasts. They have drifted here from the East End and are making some of those splendid residences impossible."

Hubert struggled into his hat and coat, and went out. It was exactly as Walker had said. Here was a fine residence with stables and greenhouses and the like, actually occupied by Whitechapel at its worst. A group of dingy children played on the lawn, and a woman with the accumulated grime of weeks on her face was hanging something that passed for washing out of an upper window. The flower beds were trampled down, a couple of attenuated donkeys browsed on the lawn.

Hubert strolled up to the house fuming. Two men were sprawling on a couple of morocco chairs smoking filthy pipes. They looked up at the newcomer with languid curiosity. They appeared quite to appreciate the fact that they were absolutely masters of the situation.

"What are you doing here?" Hubert demanded.

"If you're the owner well and good," was the reply. "If not, you take an' 'ook it. We know which side our bread's buttered."

There was nothing for it but to accept this philosophical suggestion. Hubert swallowed his rising indignation and departed. There were other evidences of the ragged invasion as he went down the road. Here and there a house was closed and the blinds down; but it was an exception rather than the rule.

Hubert walked away till he could find a cab, and was driven off to Scotland Yard in a state of indignation. The view of the matter rather startled the officials there.

"We have been so busy," the Chief Inspector said; "but the matter shall be attended to. Dr. Label was here yesterday, and at his suggestion we are having the whole force electrically treated—a kind of electrical hardening of the throat. The doctor claims that his recent treatment is as efficacious against the diphtheria as vaccination is against smallpox. It is in all the papers to-day. All London will be going mad over the new remedy to-morrow."

Hubert nodded thoughtfully. The electric treatment seemed the right thing. Label had shown him what an effect the application of the current had had on the teeming mass of matter taken from the road cutting. He thought it over until he fell asleep in his cab on the way back to his weary labours.

London raged for the new remedy. The electric treatment for throat troubles is no new thing. In this case it was simple and painless, and it had been guaranteed by one of the popular heroes of the hour. A week before Label had been regarded as a crank and a faddist; now people were ready to swear by him.

Had he not prophesied this vile disease for years, and was he not the only man who had a remedy? And the Emperor of Asturia was mending rapidly.

Had Label bidden the people to stand on their heads for an hour a day as a sovereign specific they would have done so gladly. Every private doctor and every public institution was worked to death. At the end of ten days practically all London had been treated. There was nothing for it now but to wait patiently for the result.

Another week passed and then suddenly the inrush of cases began to drop. The average at the end of the second week was down to eighty per day. On the seventeenth and eighteenth days there were only four cases altogether and in each instance they proved to be patients who had not submitted themselves to the treatment.

The scourge was over. Two days elapsed and there were no fresh cases whatever. Some time before a strong posse of police had swamped down upon Devonshire Park and cleared all the slum people out of their luxurious quarters. One or two of the bolder dwellers in that once favoured locality began to creep back. Now that they were inoculated there seemed little to fear.

But Label had something to say about that. He felt that he was free to act now, he had his royal patient practically off his hands. A strong Royal Commission had been appointed by Parliament to go at once thoroughly into the matter.

"And I am the first witness called," he chuckled to Hubert as the latter sat with the great German smoking a well-earned cigar. "I shall be able to tell a few things."

He shook his big head and smiled. The exertion of the last few weeks did not seem to have told upon him in the slightest.

"I also have been summoned," Hubert said. "But you don't suggest that those fine houses should be destroyed?"

"I don't suggest anything. I am going to confine myself to facts. One of your patent medicine advertisements says that electricity is life. Never was a truer word spoken. What has saved London from a great scourge? Electricity. What kills this new disease and renders it powerless? Electricity. And what is the great agent to fight dirt and filth with whenever it exists in great quantities? Always electricity. It has not been done before on the ground of expense, and look at the consequences. In one way and another it will cost London 2,000,000 to settle this matter. It was only a little over a third of that I asked for. Wait till you hear me talk!"

Naturally the greatest interest was taken in the early sittings of the Commission. A somewhat pompous chairman was prepared to exploit Label for his own gratification and self-glory. But the big German would have none of it. From the very first he dominated the Committee, he would give his evidence in his own way, he would speak of facts as he found them. And, after all, he was the only man there who had any practical knowledge of the subject of the inquiry.

"You would destroy the houses?" an interested member asked.

"Nothing of the kind," Label growled. "Not so much as a single pig-sty. If you ask me what electricity is I cannot tell you. It is a force in nature that as yet we don't understand. Originally it was employed as a destroyer of sewage, but it was abandoned as too expensive. You are the richest country in the world, and one of the most densely populated. Yet you are covering the land with jerry-built houses, the drainages of which will frequently want looking to. And your only way of discovering this is when a bad epidemic breaks out. Everything is too expensive. You will be a jerry-built people in a jerry-built empire. And your local authorities adopt some cheap system and then smile at the ratepayers and call for applause. Electricity will save all danger. It is dear at first, but it is far cheaper in the long run."

"If you will be so good as to get to the point," the chairman suggested.

Label smiled pityingly. He was like a schoolmaster addressing a form of little boys.

"The remedy is simple," he said. "I propose to have a couple of 10,000 volts wires discharging their current into the ground here and there over the affected area. Inoculation against the trouble is all very well, but it is not permanent and there is always danger whilst the source of it remains. I propose to remove the evil. Don't ask me what the process is, don't ask me what wonderful action takes place. All I know is that some marvellous agency gets to work and that a huge mound of live disease is rendered safe and innocent as pure water. And I want these things now, I don't want long sittings and reports and discussions. Let me work the cure and you can have all the talking and sittings you like afterwards."

Label got his own way, he would have got anything he liked at that moment. London was quiet and humble and in a mood to be generous.

Label stood over the cutting whence he had procured the original specimen of all the mischief. He was a little quiet and subdued, but his eyes shone and his hand was a trifle unsteady. His fingers trembled as he took up a fragment of the blue grey stratum and broke it up.

"Marvellous mystery," he cried. "We placed the wires in the earth and that great, silent, powerful servant has done the rest. Underground the current radiates, and, as it radiates, the source of the disease grows less and less until it ceases to be altogether. Only try this in the tainted areas of all towns and in a short time disease of all kinds would cease for ever."

"You are sure that stuff is wholesome, now?" Hubert asked.

"My future on it," Label cried. "Wait till we get it under the microscope. I am absolutely confident that I am correct."

And he was.

A BUBBLE BURST

The era of peace which seemed to be well-begun in 1906 was naturally marked by an extraordinary commercial and financial activity; an amount of world-wide speculations never equalled in intensity, even in the mad times of the South Sea Bubble, or when Hudson, the Railway King, flourished. The countless millions piled up in English banks earning a 2? per cent. interest were lavishly withdrawn, new mines had been started, everybody was going to be rich. On the face of it people had good grounds for their sanguine expectations. The Rand with its forty square miles of of rich gold-bearing reefs containing an untold number of immense fortunes—the richest region on earth—was properly administered for the first time. From the highest to the lowest everybody was investing their savings in South Africa.

In other words, there was a tremendous "boom." Nothing like it had ever been seen in the history of commerce. It was the golden hour of the promoter. Yet, for the most part, the schemes promised well. There was, however, an enormous amount of rubbish ion the market. Some of the more thoughtful financiers scented danger ahead, but they were not listened to. The roar of the Kaffir circus resounded in men's ears and made them mad. Park Lane would never be able to hold the new millionaires.

All England was in the grip of the mania. Bona fide speculation and business had become gambling pure and simple. London thought of nothing else. The City was crammed with excited buyers and operators, the little outside broker of yesterday came down to his office behind a pair of blood horses, and his diamonds were a solid sign of his new prosperity.

A busy day was drawing to a close. Carl Ericsson sat in his office smoking a cigarette. Ericsson yesterday had been waiter in an unimportant restaurant. Today he had a fine set of offices and a small mansion at Hampstead. He had "arrived" on the crest of the wave as many far less astute adventurers had done. There was a peculiarly uneasy grin on his dark features, a curious twitching of the lips, and he had the tired eyes of the sleepless.

His partner sat opposite him behind a big cigar. He was a fat man with a big jaw and a merciless mouth. Six months before Eli Smith had been a fairly well-to-do suburban butcher. Now he was E. Asherton-Smith, the big financial agent. He boasted, with truth, that he could sign a cheque for £40,000 and be none the worse for it. In the area of the City it would have been difficult to find two choicer specimens of rascality than the partners in Ericsson & Co.

"Got a big card to play, eh?" Asherton-Smith asked.

Ericsson grinned nervously. His lithe little body was quivering with excitement. There was a furtive look in his drooping eyes.

"The ace of trumps," he gurgled; "the coup of the century. Eli, my boy, how much money could we make if we could scare South Africans down five or six points for a week?"

Mr. Asherton-Smith's diamonds heaved with emotion.

"Millions," he said. "Just as many millions as we could stagger under. Makes my mouth like sawdust to think of it. But pass out a bottle of champagne."

Ericsson did so, rose from his seat and peeped into the outer office; the clerks had all gone home for the day. He closed the door gently.

"I'm going to tell you," he said. "If I don't tell someopdy I shall go mad. I can't sleep at nights for thinking of it. When I do doze off I'm sleeping in a river of sovereigns. With a bit of luck, it's a certainty."

"Get on, Carlo. You're just playing with my feelings."

"Well, it's just this way."—Ericsson's voice dropped to a whisper. "There are two lines of cable by which South Africa can communicate with the outside world—the East and West Africa cables. The West Coast line isn't to be relied upon; it breaks down at least once a week. At a time like this a breakdown is a serious matter. The directors have taken the bull by the horns, so at the present moment the West Coast line is out of our calculations. It's under repair, and it's likely to remain so for some time to come. I've ascertained that communication with South Africa by the Western line is impossible. For the next fortnight no message can come or go by that route. This leaves us only the Eastern line to grapple with. If that kindly breaks down for four-and-twenty hours, our fortunes are safe."

"Is it likely?" Asherton-Smith asked.

"Why, yes. It has happened three times during this year. I tell you I have followed this thing pretty keenly. It's more than on the cards. Suppose the breakdown did come, Eli, and we had the last message through? Look at this."

Ericsson took from a safe a sheet of paper—a cablegram message, in fact, sent out from the office of the East Africa company. It was a genuine document enough, with the date and the hour showing that it had been dispatched from Cape Town on the afternoon of the same day. There were words upon it to the effect that "Bertha has lost her aunt, and the water has been packed in the matchbox."

"That isn't our cypher," Asherton-Smith said.

"Quite right; it's the cypher used by The Messenger. The Messenger, my boy, enjoys as high a reputation as The Times. If a cablegram appeared in The Messenger tomorrow saying that there had been an earthquake on the Rand, and that the Johannesburg water-works had overflowed into the deep levels everybody could take it for gospel. That's why I managed to get hold of and learn The Messenger cypher.

"On the off-chance of the Eastern cable breaking down, I've had a cable sent to me every day from a friend in South Africa saying that there has been an earthquake in Johannesburg, and that the mines are flooded out. The cable comes to me in the cypher used by The Messenger people. That's what all that gibberish about Bertha and the water and the matchbox means.

"Suppose you were to walk into the office and say the Eastern line of cable had broken down. As the Western line is under repair that tells me that communication with South Africa is impossible for a day or more. Probably the lines would be unavailable for nearly a week. I've got a spare envelope or two used by the Eastern Company for their messages; I put this flimsy inside and alter my own address 'Bonan' to 'Bonanza'—which is the registered cable address of The Messenger—by the addition of two letters, and there you are. That's why I thought of 'Bonan' and that little office of mine in Long Lane, where I am known as James Jones.

"I've had this scheme in my mind for years. A boy drops into The Messenger office and hands over the cablegram, and there you are. The thing looks perfectly in order; it is the private cypher of the big newspaper, and, moreover, it is quite up-to-date. If the cable breaks down no questions can be asked, and the thing goes into the paper. We've only got to get the same message sent to me every day, and sooner or later our chance comes."

Asherton-Smith was breathing heavily. The prospect was dazzling. Somebody was tapping at the outer door. A large man in a big fur coat entered.

"What are you beggars conspiring about?" he asked. "Got something extra special from down below? Egad, I'd give something for a private wire of my own! We'll get a rest for a day or two. The East Africa cable is bust up south of Mauritius."

The intruder helped himself to a glass of champagne that he obviously didn't want, and drifted out again. The partners glanced at one another without speaking. Perhaps they were just a little frightened.

The thing appeared to be absolutely certain. So far as they could see, the story would be believed implicitly, for The Messenger was absolutely reliable.

The great beauty of the scheme was its conclusiveness. There had never been an earthquake on the Rand, but there was no reason why there shouldn't be. And an earthquake would assuredly destroy the Johannesburg water-works, which would mean the washing away of half the place and the flooding of some of the richest mines below the town.

The West Coast cable was under repair and incapable of use. But that frequently happened, as most people interested in South Africa knew. There was no chance of the truth trickling back to London via Australia or New York. And now the Eastern line had broken down also, as all deep sea cables do on occasion.

"Upon my word, I can't see a flaw anywhere," Ericsson remarked, in a voice that trembled. "If the Eastern line is repaired by morning we shall be none the worse off. Our coup will have miscarried, a few enquiries will be made, and James Jones will never be seen in Long Lane again."

Asherton-Smith went home and dined and drank; but sleep was not for his pillow that night. The papers were late in the morning, and that did not lessen his irritability. The breakfast stood untouched, beyond a little dry toast, and some brandy and soda water. Just for the moment the prosperous Asherton-Smith regretted the day when he had been the oily and irresponsible Eli Smith, butcher.

The papers came at last—a whole pile of them; but Asherton-Smith only desired to see The Messenger. He fluttered it open with fingers that trembled. There it was—the news that he sought. He drew a deep breath.

Usually The Messenger avoided sensation; but here was a "scoop" that no human editor could possibly resist. The headlines danced before the reader's eyes.

"Earthquake at Johannesburg. Destruction of the Water Works and the Flooding of the Mines. Great loss of life and property." The Messenger, alone of all the papers, contained this news.

A map of Johannesburg, right away from the water-works to the five-mile belt, where the world-renowned mines lay, only served to make the story more convincing. The water would have swept over the city, from the aristocratic suburb of Dorfontein to the auriferous belt that held the wealthy mines.

There were hundreds of millions of money invested here. The news of the disaster would have a depressing estate upon the Stock Exchange. Weak holders would be pretty certain to lose their heads, and the markets would be flooded with shares. Asherton-Smith trembled as he thought of his forthcoming fortune.

A little after ten o'clock he was in the City. In the train and in the streets people were talking about nothing but the great disaster in South Africa. Nobody doubted the story, although only The Messenger contained it. Unfortunately the Eastern line had broken down at a crucial moment, and no details were forthcoming for the time being. The Messenger's cable had been the last to come through.

"Going all right, eh?" Asherton-Smith asked. His teeth were chattering, but not with cold. "Pretty satisfied, eh?"

Ericsson nodded and grinned. He looked white and uneasy.

"I've started the machinery," he said. "When prices have dropped five or six points we are going to buy quietly. Mind you, I'm going to make no secret of it. I'm going to pose as the saviour of the market, the one man who refuses to bow to the panic—shall swagger about the stuff being there in spite of a dozen earthquakes.. I shall boast that at bed rock prices we can afford to buy to hold. That line will avert suspicion from us when the cat is out of the bag and our fortunes made. And you'll have to back me up on this. What a row there will be when the truth comes to be told!"

Ericsson and his partner pushed their way past inquisitive spectators who had nothing to lose, and therefore enjoyed the strange scene; they elbowed wealthy-looking men in all the garb of prosperity whose haggard faces gave the lie to their outer air.

Everybody was constrained and alert. The big financiers who usually controlled the markets were getting frightened. They assumed that there must be no panic, they desired that nothing should be done till the full magnitude of the disaster could be verified.

But people believed in the integrity of The Messenger which had never played them false yet. The great men of the exchanges and the marts had forgotten their human nature for the moment. They were asking poor humanity to put aside greed and self interest and love of money, the father to forget his savings, and the widow to ignore her dividends.. They might just as well have appealed to the common sense of a flood tide swept by the gale.

Two of the big men were penned on the pavement on Cornhill. Their names were good on "'change" for any amount in reason; they reckoned themselves rich and comfortable. But the strain of the situation was getting on their nerves.

"I'd give £50,000 to have my way here for a few hours, Henderson," said one.

"I'd give twice that to feel that I had what I deemed myself to possess yesterday," said Sir James Henderson. "What would you like to do, Kingsely?"

"Clear the streets," the great bullion broker replied. "Get some troops and Maxims, and declare the City in a state of siege for eight and-forty hours. Pass a short Act of Parliament prohibiting people from dealing in stocks and shares for a week. By that time the panic would have allayed itself and folks regained their sanity. As it is, thousands are going to be ruined. Every share in the South African market is absurdly inflated, and, even if the disaster is small, prices must keep low. But there is worse coming than that, my friend."

Already rumours were spreading far and wide as to the fall of certain shares. Mines that yesterday stood high in the estimation of the public were publicly offered at a reduction of from eight to ten points; even the gilt-edged securities were suffering.

The feeling grew that nothing was safe. It is the easiest thing in the world to shake public assurance where money is concerned. With one accord the thousands of large and small speculators had set out for the City to get rid of their liability on the earliest possible occasion. They asked for no profits, they demanded no margin—they would have been content to get out at a loss.

It never occurred to the individual that the same brilliant idea might strike a million brains simultaneously. With one accord they rushed to the line of action that might be the ruin of one-third of them. Just for the time purchases by a few bold speculators stopped the rush; but presently they got filled up or frightened so that by two o'clock some of the best paper in the market was begging at a few shillings the £1 share. When the fact struck New York and reacted on the London market, nobody knew what might happen.

It was fortunate that sellers could not unload at once. Sheaves of telegrams tumbled into brokers' offices, the floors were littered with orange envelopes, the City was musical with the tinkle of telephones. The heads of firms, half mad with worry and anxiety, were offering the girls in the telephone exchange large sums to connect them with this office and the other. The usually sane City of London was as mad now as it had been in the days of the South Sea Bubble.

By three o'clock, however, business on the Stock Exchange had practically come to a standstill. It was useless to deal with waste paper. To-morrow the crowd would doubtless be augmented by thousands of provincial speculators. Already the foreign Bourses were suffering under the strain. Early in the afternoon there were rumours and signs of an excited struggle in Lothbury.

What had happened now? People were straining their ears to listen. The news came in presently. There was a run on the South African Industrial Bank!

When the crowd began to clamour at the doors of the South African Industrial, the manager slipped out by a side entrance and made the best pace he could in the direction of the Bank of England. Once there, all his self-possession deserted him. He asked wildly to see the chief cashier, the general manager, the governors, anybody who might help him for the moment.

But the officials had other things to occupy their attention. From all parts of the country intelligence had arrived to the effect that the panic was at its height. It was only now that the big financiers realised what a large amount of fanatical gambling there had been in South Africans. Everybody had been going to make their fortunes, from humble clerks up to the needy aristocrats. Every penny that could be raked together had gone that way.

And now the country had taken it into its head that the Rand was lost. Wild appeals had been made to the Eastern Cable Company to do something, but they could only reply that their line had broken down somewhere beyond Mauritius, and that, until it could be fished up and spliced, South Africa might as well be in the moon. People were acting as if the Rand had been swallowed up altogether.

The Bank of England was full of great financiers at their wits' ends for some means of allaying the panic and restoring public confidence. The great houses, Rothschild, and Coutts, and the rest, were represented in the governor's parlour.

The presiding genius of the South African Industrial found his way into the meeting. He was sorry to trouble them; he would not have come unless he had been absolutely bound to. But there was a run on his bank, and he wanted £2,000,000 immediately. As to security—

One of the grave financiers laughed aloud. It seemed an awful thing to do in that solemn and decorous parlour, but nobody seemed to notice. But there was a general concensus of opinion that the money must be forthcoming. If one sound bank was allowed to topple over, goodness only knew where the catastrophe might end.

"You will have to do with £500,000 for the present," the chairman said. "There are sure to be other applications. You must be diplomatic; festina lente, you know."

"If I could keep open straight away until—"

"Madness. Keep to your regulations. Close at four o'clock. Delay is everything."

The manager of the South African Industrial fought his way back to the offices with a little comfort at the back of his mind.

There was a lull as he appeared. He took advantage of it. His courage had come back to him now.

"Close the doors," he said sharply. "It is past four o'clock."

The mob yelled its protest. A big man climbed over the trellis along the counter. Just for a moment it looked like a lawless riot, but a cashier whipped a revolver out from a drawer, and as the big man looked down the blue bore his courage failed him. There was no further rush, but at the same time there was disposition on the part of the crowd to retire.

"We are closed for the day," the manager said with considerable coolness. "You can't expect me to stay here all night merely because you have taken it into your heads to want your money all at once. Come tomorrow and you shall all be paid."

A derisive howl followed, The manager whispered something to one of the clerks and the latter slipped out. Presently there was a commotion at the doors, and half-a-dozen helmets topped the crowd. There was a swaying movement till the long counter creaked again, an oath or two, uplifted sticks and the smashing of a policeman's helmet.

For the next few minutes there was something in the nature of a free fight;' blows were freely exchanged, and more than one face bore traces of blood. But there is always something besides physical force behind law and order, and gradually the mob turned back. Gradually the counting-house was cleared and the iron shutters let down.

But the city did not clear. The wildest rumours were in the air. Other banks, doing a more or less large business in the way of withdrawals, had followed the example of the South African Industrial, and this had not tended to restore public confidence. It was pretty clear that every house would have to face a similar run on the morrow.

At eight o'clock the streets were still crowded. It was fairly warm; there was little or no traffic after dusk, and it became evident that thousands of people had all tacitly resolved to do the same thing— remain in the streets all night outside their particular offices or business houses, and wait so that they might have the first chance in the morning. People sat on the paths and in the roadway. Every City house of refreshment had been depleted of food long since.

Under the big electric lamps people reclined, reading the evening papers. It was a gigantic picnic, with tragedy to crown the feast. There was no laughter, nothing but grim determination of purpose.

The papers were full of bad news from the provinces. Everywhere public credit was shaken to breaking point. There had been runs on scores of local banks.

In the West-End there was only one topic of conversation. But the theatres and restaurants were open, and life was going on much the same. In a private room at the Savoy Ericsson and his partner in guilt were dining. The waiters had gone, the wine and cigars stood on the table.

There was a subdued look about both of them, a furtive cast of the eyes and just a suggestion of slackness in their hands not due entirely to the champagne. It was a long time before either of them spoke.

"Pretty warm day, Eli," Ericsson suggested.

Asherton-Smith wiped his red damp forehead.

"Rather," he said. "I'm not so sharp as you, I know, but I'd forfeit a few thousands to be well out of this."

"Ericsson was not so contemptuous of his thick-witted partner as usual.

"I should like to know what you are driving at," he muttered.

"Well, we've been too sharp. We've played the game too far. Shares were only to drop a few points, and we were to buy for the rise. And what have we got? Some hundreds of thousands of shares a few points below par? Not a bit of it. If this panic waits two days longer we shall have exchanged all our own cash and our own credit for a ton or two of waste paper."

"It will all come back again." Ericsson said uneasily.

"Ah, but when? The bogey has been too big for the public. We've given them a scare that they will not get over in a hurry for many a day. We've shown them what might happen. And they tumble to the fact that things are far too inflated. The fall of a few points would have put millions into our pockets. As it is, we shall have to hold on perhaps for months. And we're not strong enough to do that."

"If the cable works again to-morrow." Ericsson said hoarsely after a pause "it—"

"Yes, and if it doesn't? And if the thing goes on, what then? And if there should be a run to-morrow on the Bank of England!"

Ericsson and Asherton-Smith were still sipping their brandy, but they were no longer gloating over their prey with shining eyes—they no longer counted their prospective millions. Like the greedy fox they had dropped the substance for the shadow. They were going to be ruined with their victims.

With moody, furtive, bloodshot eyes they looked at each other.

"I suppose we can't drop a hint," Ericsson suggested.

"Drop a hint," Asherton-Smith sneered. "You're a clever chap, you are—too clever by half. But if that's all the idea you've got you'd better shut up. Perhaps you'd like to go and tell the story to the Lord Mayor?"

Ericsson's fine turn for repartee seemed to have deserted him.

"Who could have anticipated anything like this?" he groaned. "And the worst of it is that we dare not say a word. The merest hint would invite suspicion, and you may be pretty sure that they would make the punishment fit the crime. We'll just have to grin and bear it."

Asherton-Smith shook his fist in the speaker's face.

"You miserable swindler!" he yelled. "But for you I should have been a rich man to-day. And now I am ruined—ruined!"

Ericsson bent his head meekly with never a word to say.

The City was awake earlier than usual next morning; indeed, for once, it had not slept. By nine o'clock in the morning the streets were packed. The haggard-eyed, sleepless ones gained nothing by their tenacity, for they were pushed from pillar to post by others fresh for the fray.

The provincial trains from an early hour had commenced to pour fresh forces into London. A great many business men had slept as best they could in their offices, feeling pretty sure that it was the only way to be on the spot in the morning. They looked tired and worn out.

It was a quiet, persistent grim crowd. There was no hustling or horse- play, or anything of that kind; even the ubiquitous humourist was absent. They pushed on persistently, a denser crowd round the large banks. As soon as the shutters were down and the doors opened the human tide streamed in.

The run on the banks had set in grimly. Clerks and cashiers from distant branches had been brought up to meet the pressure.

There was a confidence in the way they bustled about and handled and paid out the money that was not without its effect. More than one man eyed the pile of notes in his hand and passed them back over the counter again. Here and there people were bewailing the loss of their money.

It was the golden hour of the light-fingered fraternity. They were absolutely covered by the dense crowd so that they could pursue their vocation with impunity. They had only to mark down some rich prize and plunder. Individuals shrieked that they had been robbed, but nobody took any notice.

A burley, red-faced farmer yelled that he had been robbed of £800 in Bank of England notes. Someone by him retorted that it was no loss, seeing that there was a run on the great National bank.

A run on the Bank of England!
It was the thrilling moment of the day! A run on the Bank of England! And yet it seemed in the light of new circumstances to be the most natural thing in the world. Would the bank be able to cash its own notes? If not—well, if not—nobody could foresee the end.

There were thousands of curious people in the crowd who had no business there whatever. Not that there was any business properly so called done in London that day. There was a surging rush in the direction of Threadneedle Street. It would be something in after life to say that one had seen a run on the Bank of England.

Inside the paying departments huge piles of gold and silver glittered in the sunshine. It was a curious and thrilling contrast between the grave decorum of the clerks and the wild, fierce rush of the public.

The piles of gold and the easy unconcern of the officials satisfied a good many people who pushed to the counters and then fell back again muttering uncomfortably; but, in real truth, the bank managers were becoming a little anxious.

Lord Fairchild, the great capitalist, with his houses in every big city of the world, contrived at length to reach the bank parlour. There was a full meeting of the chairman and governors. A cheerful tone prevailed.

"I sincerely hope we may weather the storm," the chairman said anxiously. "We have had no signal of distress from anyone; but I shall be glad when it is over."

Everybody looked tired and worn out. One or two of the governors had fallen asleep in their chairs. There was a litter of lunch on the table. But very few of those assembled there seemed to care anything for food.

"I calculate that we can last another day," Lord Fairchild said. "By to-morrow I hope we shall have contact with Cape Town again."

Every effort was being made to bring about this desirable consummation. The broken line might be repaired at any moment. News had come from the Mauritius that the broken cable had been fished up, but there was no further information since midnight. Possibly, when contact could be made again, the disaster would prove to be much less than the last message had forecasted.

"It must come soon," one of the governors sighed, "It must come soon, or Parliament will have to deal with this question. Another two days—"

"I prefer not to think of another two days," Lord Fairchild replied. "If the worse comes to the worst, Government must guarantee our paper. We shall have to issue Treasury bills to make up our deficit. We—"

An excited individual burst without ceremony into the room. His hat was off; his smart frock coat was torn to ribands.

"I am from the office of the East Cable Company," he gasped "I was told to come here at once. My lord, I have the most extraordinary news. The great disaster at Johannesburg is—is—is—"

"Get on man; we are all impatience."

"Is—is no disaster at all. We have verified it. Our agent at Cape Town says he has heard nothing of it. Johannesburg stands where it did. There are four messages through and—well, there has been a cruel fraud, and we are doing our best to get to the bottom of it."

A rousing cheer echoed through the bank parlour. The governors yelled and shook each other by the hand like school-boys. Probably the decorum of that room had never been so grossly violated before.

Lord Fairchild passed into the great office where the public were still pushing and struggling. He stood on a table, his spare and striking figure standing out conspicuously. There were hundreds present who recognised that noble figure.

"Gentlemen," Lord Fairchild cried. "I have just received the most authentic information that Johannesburg stands intact to-day. There has been trickery somewhere, but, thank Heaven, the panic is over."

A perfect yell followed. Men went frantic with delight. When Lord Fairchild said a thing it was accepted as gospel. Hats went high in the air, people shook hands with perfect strangers, there was a rush to pay gold back and take notes instead.

The news spread in the marvellous magnetic way common to the ear of a huge multitude. It ran with lightning speed through the streets. Everybody seemed to know like magic that Lord Fairchild had made a short speech in the Bank of England to the effect that the scare was over. In less than ten minutes the various bank officials were deeply engaged in taking back again the piles of gold they had so recently paid out. The mob roared out patriotic songs, there was a rush in all directions. For the next hour or so the telegraph lines fairly hummed with messages. Within an hour the City had regained much of its usual busy decorum, save for the long stream of people who were getting rid of their gold once more.

With a view to prevent any further exploiting and financial uneasiness on the part of the speculating fraternity the commitee of the Stock Exchange met and formally closed the House till Monday. Under the circumstances the step was an exceedingly wise one.

In the seclusion of the bank parlour Lord Fairchild was closeted with the editor of The Messenger. He had come down post haste to the City to vindicate his character. The famous cablegram lay on the table.

"I need not say, my lord," he began, "that I—"

"You need not say anything about yourself," Lord Fairchild said kindly "We are quite convinced that you have been made a victim. But how?"

"I can only theorise at present," the Messenger editor replied. "And you, gentlemen, will understand, a great newspaper like ours has correspondants everywhere. We also have a special cypher known only to ourselves. Our man at the Cape is absolutely reliable. Now somebody must have stolen our cypher or possessed himself of the key. Cables come to us adressed to 'Bonanza.' Such was the cable that reached us on the day that the Eastern line broke down. Seeing that it was absolutely in order and apparently delivered in the usual way, we used it, under the impression that we had a great piece of news and one that possibly our rivals did not possess."

"There was nothing in the appearance of the cablegram to excite our suspicions, but since the news of its falseness has come through I have had it examined by an expert who reports that the original telegram had been directed to 'Bonan,' and not to 'Bonanza.' The last two letters had been cleverly forged, but under a very strong glass the forgery is clear. Now you can see the trap. I have been to the office of the Cable Company, and, as I expected, I find that a message was sent on the day in question from Cape Town to a registered 'Bonan'. This 'Bonan' turns out to be one James Jones who has an office in Long Lane. Of course that office was taken for the express purpose of getting that message, so that in case the Eastern line broke down the paper could be forced upon us. Unfortunately it was forced upon us with dire results. We find that the message was repeated day by day in the hopes of a breakdown.

"Now, lots of big houses down South cable quotations, lists of prices, finds of gold-dust and the like every day. All these are in cypher, and perhaps a fortnight might pass without any fluctuations, which would mean practically the receipt of an identical message for days. Nothing but a close search of the records could have aroused suspicion. Besides, the line had broken down, and all the energies of the company were devoted to that.

"If any of you gentlemen like to call at the Cable Company's offices and see the scores of duplicate cypher messages, all more or less alike, you will be convinced that the employees there are not in the least at fault. We have been the victims of a clever conspiracy. We can safely leave the rest to the police."

The City was becoming normal again. By four o'clock it was practically deserted. The offices of the various banks were bursting with the repaid gold. Many clerks were closing up the books and looking forward to a good night's rest.

It was almost impossible to believe that these were the same streets of a few hours before.

Meantime, Ericsson and his partner in the inner room of their offices were gloating over a bewildering array of figures; their gains from the gigantic hoax they had played on the public promised to run into millions.

Rejoicing in the sudden turn in affairs, the two guilty men were building castles in the air with their ill-gotten wealth, when heavy footsteps came up from the office stairs; there was a knocking at the door The two men started up. Their nerves were humming still from the strain of the past day and night.

"Come in," Asherton-Smith cried unsteadily.

A couple of men entered. One of them had a paper in his hand.

"Mr. Asherton-Smith and Mr. Carl Ericsson, alias James Jones," he said, "I have a warrant for your arrest which I will read to you presently. I warn you not to say too much. Your accomplice, Jacob Peters, has been arrestcd at Cape Town and I am instructed by cable that he has made a full confession."

The snarling oath died away on Ericsson's lips.

"It's all up," he said hoarsely, "but it was a chance. Curse Peters for a white-livered fool. But for him I should be worth fifty millions."

THE INVISIBLE FORCE

I

It seemed as if London had solved one of her great problems at last. The communication difficulty was at an end. The first-class ticket- holders no longer struggled to and from business with fourteen fellow-sufferers in a third-class carriage. There were no longer any particularly favoured suburbs, nor were there isolated localities where it took as long getting to the City as an express train takes between London and Swindon. The pleasing paradox of a man living at Brighton because it was nearer to his business than Surbiton had ceased to exist. The tubes had done away with all that.

There were at least a dozen hollow cases running under London in all directions. They were cool and well ventilated, the carriages were brilliantly lighted, the various loops were properly equipped and managed.

All day long the shining funnels and bright platforms were filled with passengers. Towards midnight the traffic grew less, and by half-past one o'clock the last train had departed. The all-night service was not yet.

It was perfectly quiet now along the gleaming core that lay buried under Bond Street and St. James's Street, forming the loop running below the Thames close by Westminster Bridge Road and thence to the crowded Newington and Walworth districts. Here a portion of the roof was under repair.

The core was brilliantly lighted; there was no suggestion of fog or gloom. The general use of electricity had disposed of a good deal of London's murkiness; electric motors were applied now to most manufactories and workshops. There was just as much gas consumed as ever, but it was principally used for heating and culinary purposes. Electric radiators and cookers had not yet reached the multitude; that was a matter of time.

In the flare of the blue arc lights a dozen men were working on the dome of the core. Something had gone wrong with a water-main overhead, the concrete beyond the steel belt had cracked, and the moisture had corroded the steel plates, so that a long strip of the metal skin had been peeled away, and the friable concrete had fallen on the rails. It had brought part of the crown with it, so that a maze of large and small pipes was exposed to view.

"They look like the reeds of an organ," a raw engineer's apprentice remarked to the foreman. "What are they?"

"Gas mains, water, electric light, telephone, goodness knows what," the foreman replied. "They branch off here, you see."

"Fun to cut them," the apprentice grinned. The foreman nodded absently. He had once been a mischievous boy, too. The job before him looked a bigger thing than he had expected. It would have to be patched up till a strong gang could be turned on to the work. The raw apprentice was still gazing at the knot of pipes. What fun it would be to cut that water-main and flood the tunnels!

In an hour the scaffolding was done and the debris cleared away. To-morrow night a gang of men would come and make the concrete good and restore the steel rim to the dome. The tube was deserted. It looked like a polished, hollow needle, lighted here and there by points of dazzling light.

It was so quiet and deserted that the falling of a big stone reverberated along the tube with a hollow sound. There was a crack, and a section of piping gave way slightly and pressed down upon one of the electric mains. A tangled skein of telephone wires followed. Under the strain the electric cable parted and snapped. There was a long, sliding, blue flame, and instantly the tube was in darkness. A short circuit had been established somewhere. Not that it mattered, for traffic was absolutely suspended now, and would not be resumed again before daylight. Of course, there were the workmen's very early trains, and the Covent Garden market trains, but they did not run over this section of the line. The whole darkness reeked with the whiff of burning indiarubber. The moments passed on drowsily.

Along one side of Bond Street the big lamps were out. All the lights on one main switch had gone. But it was past one o'clock now, and the thing mattered little. These accidents occurred sometimes in the best regulated districts, and the defect would be made good in the morning.

It was a little awkward, though, for a great State ball was in progress at Buckingham Palace. Supper was over, the magnificent apartments were brilliant with light dresses and gay uniforms. The shimmer and fret of diamonds flashed back to lights dimmer than themselves. There was a slide of feet over the polished floors. Then, as if some unseen force had cut the bottom of creation, light and gaiety ceased to be, and darkness fell like a curtain.

There were a few cries of alarm from the swift suddenness of it. To eyes accustomed to that brilliant glow the gloom was Egyptian. It seemed as if some great catastrophe had happened. But common-sense reasserted itself, and the brilliant gathering knew that the electric light had failed.

There were quick commands, and spots of yellow flame sprang out here and there in the great desert of the night. How faint and feeble, and yellow and flaring, the lights looked! The electrician down below was puzzled, for, so far as he could see, the fuses in the meters were intact. There was no short circuit so far as the Palace was concerned. In all probability there had been an accident at the generating stations; in a few minutes the mischief would be repaired.

But time passed, and there was no welcome return of the flood of crystal light.

"It is a case for all the candles," the Lord Chamberlain remarked; "fortunately the old chandeliers are all fitted. Light the candles."

It was a queer, grotesque scene, with all that wealth of diamonds and glitter of uniforms and gloss of satins, under the dim suggestion of the candles. And yet it was enjoyable from the very novelty of it. Nothing could be more appropriate for the minuet that was in progress.

"I feel like one of my own ancestors," a noble lord remarked. "When they hit upon that class of candle I expect they imagined that the last possibility in the way of lighting had been accomplished. Is it the same outside, Sir George?"

Sir George Egerton laughed. He was fresh from the gardens.

"It's patchwork," he said. "So far as I can judge, London appears to be lighted in sections. I expect there is a pretty bad breakdown. My dear chap, do you mean to say that clock is right?"

"Half-past four, sure enough, and mild for the time of year. Did you notice a kind of rumbling under— Merciful Heavens, what is that?"

II

There was a sudden splitting crack as if a thousand rifles had been discharged in the ballroom. The floor rose on one side to a perilous angle, considering the slippery nature of its surface. Such a shower of white flakes fell from the ceiling that dark dresses and naval uniforms looked as if their wearers had been out in a snowstorm.

One of the great crystal chandeliers was falling
Cracks and fissures started in the walls with pantomimic effect, on all sides could be heard the rattle and splinter of falling glass. A voice suddenly uprose in a piercing scream, a yell proclaimed that one of the great crystal chandeliers was falling. There was a rush and a rustle of skirts, and a quick vision of white, beautiful faces, and with a crash the great pendant came to the floor.

The whole world seemed to be oscillating under frightened feet, the palace was humming and thrumming like a harpstring. The panic was so great, the whole mysterious tragedy so sudden, that the bravest there had to battle for their wits. Save for a few solitary branches of candles, the big room was in darkness.

There were fifteen hundred of England's bravest, and fairest, and best, huddled together in what might be a hideous deathchamber for all they knew to the contrary. Women were clinging in terror to the men, the fine lines of class distinction were broken down. All were poor humanity now in the presence of a common danger.

In a little time the earth ceased to sway and rock, the danger was passing. A little colour was creeping back to the white faces again. Men and women were conscious that they could hear the beating of their own hearts. Nobody broke the silence yet, for speech seemed to be out of place.

"An earthquake," somebody said at length. "An earthquake, beyond doubt, and a pretty bad one at that. That accounts for the failure of the electric light. There will be some bad accidents if the gas mains are disturbed."

The earth grew steady underfoot again, the white flakes ceased to fall. Amongst the men the spirit of adventure was rising; the idea of standing quietly there and doing nothing was out of the question.

Anyway, there could be no further thought of pleasure that night. There were many mothers there, and their uppermost thought was for home. Never, perhaps, in the history of royalty had there been so informal a breaking up of a great function. The King and Queen had retired some little time before—a kindly and thoughtful act under the circumstances. The women were cloaking and shawling hurriedly; they crowded out in search of their carriages with no more order than would have been obtained outside a theatre.

But there were remarkably few carriages in waiting. An idiotic footman who had lost his head in the sudden calamity sobbed out the information that Oxford Street and Bond Street were impassable, and that houses were down in all directions. No vehicles could come that way; the road was destroyed. As to the rest, the man knew nothing; he was frightened out of his life.

There was nothing for it but to walk. It wanted two good hours yet before dawn, but thousands of people seemed to be abroad. For a space of a mile or more there was not a light to be seen. Round Buckingham Palace the atmosphere reeked with a fine irritating dust, and was rendered foul and poisonous by the fumes of coal gas. There must have been a fearful leakage somewhere.

Nobody seemed to know what was the matter, and everybody was asking everybody else. And in the darkness it was very hard to locate the disaster. Generally, it was admitted, that London had been visited by a dreadful earthquake. Never were the daylight hours awaited more eagerly.

"The crack of doom," Sir George Egerton remarked to his companion, Lord Barcombe.

They were feeling their way across the park in the direction of the Mall.

"It's like a shuddering romance that I read a little time since. But I must know something about it before I go to bed. Let's try St. James's Street—if there's any St. James Street left."

"All right," Lord Barcombe agreed, "I hope the clubs are safe. Is it wise to strike a match with all this gas reeking in the air?"

"Anything's better than the gas," Sir George said tersely.

The vesta flared out in a narrow, purple circle. Beyond it was a glimpse of a seat with two or three people huddled on it. They were outcasts and companions in the grip of misfortune, but they were all awake now.

"Can any of you say what's happened?" Lord Barcombe asked.

"The world's come to an end, sir, I believe," was the broken reply. "You may say what you like, but it was a tremendous explosion. I saw a light like all the world ablaze over to the north, and then all the lights went out, and I've been waiting for the last trump to sound ever since."

"Then you didn't investigate?" Lord Barcombe asked.

"Not me, sir. I seem to have struck a bit of solid earth where I am. And then it rained stones and pieces of brick and vestiges of creation. There's the half of a boiler close to you that dropped out of the sky. You stay where you are, sir."

But the two young men pushed on. They reached what appeared to be St. James's Street at length, but only by stumbling and climbing over heaps of debris.

The roadway was one mass of broken masonry. The fronts of some of the clubs had been stripped off as if a titanic knife had sliced them. It was like looking into one of the upholsterers' smart shops, where they display rooms completely furnished. There were gaps here and there where houses had collapsed altogether. Seeing that the road had ceased to exist, it seemed impossible that an earthquake could have done this thing. A great light flickered and roared a little way down the road. At an angle a gas main was tilted up like the spout of a teapot, upheaved and snapped from its twin pipes. This had caught fire in some way, so that for a hundred yards or so each way the thoroughfare was illuminated by a huge flare lamp.

It was a thrilling sight focused in that blue glare. It looked as if London had been utterly destroyed by a siege—as if thousands of well- aimed shells had exploded. Houses looked like tattered banners of brick and mortar. Heavy articles of furniture had been hurled into the street; on the other hand, little gimcrack ornaments still stood on tiny brackets.

A scared-looking policeman came staggering along.

"My man," Lord Barcombe cried, "what has happened?"

The officer pulled himself together and touched his helmet.

"It's dreadful, sir," he sobbed. "There has been an accident in the tubes; and they have been blown all to pieces."

III

The constable, for the moment, had utterly lost his nerve. He stood there in the great flaring roar of the gas mains with a dazed expression that was pitiful.

"Can you tell us anything about it?" Lord Barcombe asked.

"I was in Piccadilly," was the reply. "Everything was perfectly quiet and so far as I could see not a soul was in sight. Then I heard a funny rushing sound, just like the tear of an express train through a big, empty station. Yes, it was for all the world like a ghostly express train that you could hear and not see. It came nearer and nearer; the whole earth trembled just as if the train had gone mad in Piccadilly. It rushed past me down St. James's Street, and after that there was an awful smash and a bang, and I was lying on my back in the middle of the road. All the lights that remained went out, and for a minute or two I was in that railway collision. Then, when I got my senses back, I blundered down here because of that big flaring light there; and I can't tell you, gentlemen, any more, except that the tube has blown up."

Of that fact there was no question. There were piles of debris thrown high in one part and a long deep depression in another like a ruined dyke. A little further on the steel core of the tube lay bare with rugged holes ripped in it.

"Some ghastly electric catastrophe," Sir George Egerton murmured.

It was getting light by this time, and it was possible to form some idea of the magnitude of the disaster. Some of the clubs in St James's Street still appeared to be intact, but others had suffered terribly. The heaps of tumbled masonry were powdered and glittering with broken glass and a few walls hung perilously over the pavement. And still the gas main roared on until the flame grew from purple to violet, and to straw colour before the coming dawn. If this same thing had happened all along the network of tubes London would be more or less a hideous ruin.

For the better part of Piccadilly things were brighter. Evidently the explosion had had a straight run here, for the road had been raised like some mighty zigzag molehill for many yards. The wood pavement scattered all over the place suggested a gigantic box of child's bricks strewn over a nursery floor. The tube had been forced up, its outer envelope of concrete broken so that the now twisted steel core might have been a black snake crawling down Piccadilly. Doubtless the expanding air had met with some obstacle in the tube under St. James's Street, hence the terrible force of the explosion there.

There was quite a large crowd in Oxford Street. The whole roadway was wet; the gutters ran with the water from the broken pipes. The air was full of the odour of gas. All the clocks in the streets seemed to have gone mad. Lord Barcombe glanced at his own watch, to find that it was racing furiously.

"By Jove!" he whispered excitedly, "we're in danger here. The air is full of electricity. I went over some works once and neglected to leave my watch behind me, and it played me the same prank. It affects the mainspring, you know."

There were great ropes and coils of electric wire of high voltage cropping out of the ground here and there; coils attached to huge accumulators, and discharging murderous current freely. A dog, picking his way across the sopping street, trod on one of the wires, and instantly all that remained of the dog was what looked like a twisted bit of burnt skin and bone. It appealed to Sir George Egerton's imagination strongly.

"Poor little brute!" he murmured. "It might have happened to you or me. Don't you know that a force that only gives a man a bad shock when he is standing on dry ground often kills him when the surface is wet? I wonder if we can get some indiarubber gloves and galoshes hereabouts. After that gruesome sight, I shall be afraid to put one foot before the other."

Indeed, the precaution was a necessary one. A horse attached to a cab came creeping over the blocked streets; the animal slipped on a grating connected with the ventilation of the drains, and a fraction of a second later there was no horse in existence. The driver sat on his perch, white and scared.

"The galoshes," Lord Barcombe said hoarsely. "Don't you move till we come back again, my man. And everybody keep out of the roadway."

The cry ran along that the roadway meant instant death. The cabman sat there gibbering with terror. A little way further down was a rubber warehouse, with a fine selection of waders' and electricians' gloves in the window. With a fragment of concrete Sir George smashed in the window, and took what he and Lord Barcombe required. They knew that they would be quite safe now.

More dead than alive the cabman climbed down from his seat and was carried to the pavement on Lord Barcombe's shoulder. The left side of his face was all drawn up and puckered, the left arm was useless.

"Apoplexy from the fright," Sir George suggested.

"Not a bit of it," Lord Barcombe exclaimed, "It's a severe electric shock. Hold up."

Gradually the man's face and arm ceased to twitch.

"If that's being struck by lightning," he said, "I don't want another dose. It was as if something had caught hold of me and frozen my heart in my body. I couldn't do a thing. And look at my coat."

All up the left side the coat was singed so that at a touch the whole cloth fell to pieces. It was a strange instance of the freakishness of the invisible force. A great fear fell on those who saw. This intangible, unseen danger, with its awful swiftness, was worse than the worse that could be seen.

"Let's get home," Lord Barcombe suggested. "It's getting on my nerves. It's dreadful when all the terror is left to the imagination."

IV

Meanwhile no time was lost in getting to the root of the mischief.

The danger could not be averted by switching off the power altogether at the various electrical stations of the metropolis. At intervals along the tubes were immense accumulators which for the present could not be touched. It was these accumulators that rendered the streets such a ghastly peril.

It was the electrical expert to the County Council—Alton Rossiter— who first got on the track of the disaster. More than once before, the contact between gas and electricity had produced minor troubles of this kind. Gas that had escaped into man-holes and drains had been fired from the sparks caused by a short-circuit current wire. For some time, even as far back as 1895, instances of this kind had been recorded.

But how could the gas have leaked into the tube, seeing that it was a steel core with a solid bedding of concrete beyond? Unless an accident had happened when the tube was under repair, this seemed impossible.

The manager of the associated tubes was quite ready to afford every information to Mr. Rossiter. The core had corroded in Bond Street in consequence of a settling of the earth caused by a leaky water-main. The night before, this had been located and the steel skin stripped off for the necessary repairs.

Mr. Alton Rossiter cut the speaker short.

"Will you come to Bond Street with me, Mr. Fergusson?" he said; "we may be able to get into the tunnel there."

Fergusson was quite ready. The damage in Bond Street was not so great, though the lift shaft was filled with debris, and it became necessary to cut a way into the station before the funnel was reached.

For a couple of hundred yards the tube was intact; beyond that point the fumes of gas were overpowering. A long strip of steel hung from the roof. Just where it was, a round, clean hole in the roadway rendered it possible to work and breathe there in spite of the gas fumes.

"We shall have to manage as best we can," Rossiter muttered. "For a little time at any rate, the gas of London must be cut of entirely. With broken mains all over the place the supply is positively dangerous. Look here."

He pointed to the spot where the gas main had trended down and where a short-circuit wire had fused it. Here was the whole secret in a nutshell. A roaring gas main had poured a dense volume into the tube for hours; mixed with the air it had become one of the most powerful and deadly of explosives.

"What time does your first train start?" Rossiter asked.

"For the early markets, four o'clock," Fergusson replied. "In other words, we switch on the current from the accumulator stations at twenty minutes to four."

"And this is one of your generating stations?"

"Yes. Of course I see exactly what you are driving at. Practically the whole circuit of tubes was more or less charged with a fearful admixture of gas and air. As soon as the current was switched on a spark exploded the charge. I fear, I very much fear, that you are right. If we can only find the man in charge here! But that would be nothing else than a miracle."

All the same the operator in charge of the switches was close by. Fortunately for him the play of the current in the tube had carried the gases towards St. James's Street. The explosion had lifted him out of his box, and for a time he lay stunned. Dazed and confused, he had climbed to the street and staggered into the shop of a chemist who was just closing the door upon a customer who had rung him up for a prescription.

But he could say very little. There had been an explosion directly he pulled down the first of the switches, and his memory was a blank after that.

Anyway, the cause of the disaster was found. To prevent further catastrophe notice was immediately given to the various gas companies to cut off the supplies at once. In a little time the whole disastrous length of the tube was free from that danger.

By the afternoon a committee had gone over the whole route. At the first blush it looked as if London had been half ruined. It was impossible yet to estimate the full extent of the damage. In St. James's Street alone the loss was pretty certain to run into millions.

Down in Whitehall and Parliament Street, and by Westminster Bridge, the damage was terrible. Here sharp curves and angles had checked the rush of expanding air with the most dire results. Huge holes and ruts had been made in the earth, and houses had come down bodily.

Most of the people out in the streets by this time were properly equipped in indiarubber shoes and gloves. It touched the imagination strongly to know that between a man and hideous death was a thin sheet of rubber no thicker than a shilling. It was like walking over the crust of a slumbering volcano; like skating at top speed over very thin ice.

Towards the evening a thrilling whisper ran round. From Deptford two early specials had started to convey an annual excursion of five hundred men and their wives to Paddington, whence they were going to Windsor. It seemed impossible, incredible, that these could have been overlooked; but by five o'clock the dreadful truth was established. Those two specials had started; but what oblivion they had found—how lingering, swift, or merciful, nobody could tell.

V

There was a new horror. The story of those early special trains gave the final terror to the situation. Probably they had been blown to eternity. There was just one chance in a million that anybody had escaped. All the same something would have to be done to put the matter at rest.

Nobody knew what to do; everybody had lost their heads for the moment. It seemed hopeless from the very start. Naturally, the man that everybody looked to at the moment was Fergusson of the associated tubes. With him was Alton Rossiter, representing the County Council.

"But how to make a start?" the latter asked.

"We will start from Deptford," said Fergusson. "We must first ascertain the exact time that the train left Deptford, and the precise moment when the first explosion took place. Mind you, I believe there was a series of explosions. You see, there is always a fair amount of air in the tubes. When the inflowing gas met the cross currents of air, it would be diverted, or pocketed, so to speak. We should have a big pocket of the explosive, followed by a clear space.

"When the switches were turned on there would be sparks here and there all along the tubes. This means that practically simultaneously the mines would be fired; fired so quickly that the series of reports would sound like one big bang. That this must be so can be seen by the state of some of the streets. In some spots the tube has been wrenched bodily from the earth as easily as if it had been a gaspipe. And then, again, you have streets that do not show the slightest damage. You must agree with me that my theory is a correct one."

"I do. But what are you driving at?"

"Well, I am afraid that my theory is a very forlorn one, but I give it for what it is worth. It's just possible, faintly possible, that those trains ran into a portion of the tube where there was no explosion at all. There were explosions behind them and in front of them, and of course the machinery would have been rendered useless instantly, so that the trains may be trapped with no ingress or outlet. I'm not in the least sanguine of finding anything, but the aftermath of a fearful tragedy. Anyway, our duty is pretty plainly before us—we must go to Deptford. Come along."

The journey to Deptford was no easy one. There were so many streets up that locomotion was a difficult matter. And where the streets were damaged there was danger. It was possible to use cycles, seeing that the rubber tires formed non-conductors, and indiarubber gloves and shoes allowed extra protection. But the mere suggestion of a spill was thrilling. It might mean the tearing of a glove or the loss of a shoe, and then—well, that did not bear thinking about.

"I never before properly appreciated the feelings of the man that Blondin used to carry on his back," Rossiter said as the pair pushed steadily through Bermondsey, "but I can understand his emotions now."

The roads, even where there was no danger, were empty. A man or woman would venture timidly out and look longingly to the other side of the road and then give up the idea of moving altogether. As a matter of fact there was more of it safe than otherwise, but the risks were too awful.

VI

Meanwhile something like an organised attempt was being made to grapple with the evil: Days must, of necessity, elapse before a proper estimate of the damage could be made, to say nothing of the loss of life.

Nothing very great could be accomplished, however, until the huge accumulators ha been cleared and the deadly current switched off. So far as the London area proper was concerned, Holborn Viaduct was the point to aim at. In big vaults there, underground, were some of the largest accumulators in the world. These would have to be rendered harmless at any cost.

But the work was none so easy, seeing that the tube here was crushed and twisted, and all about it was a knot of high-pressure cables deadly to the touch. There was enough power here running to waste to destroy a city. There were spaces that it was impossible to cross; and unfortunately the danger could not be seen. There was no warning, no chance of escape for the too hardy adventurer; he would just have stepped an inch beyond the region of safety, and there would have been an end of him. No wonder that the willing workers hesitated.

There was nothing for it but the blasting of the tube. True, this might be attended with danger to such surrounding buildings as had weathered the storm, but it was the desperate hour for desperate remedies. A big charge of dynamite rent a long slit in the exposed length of tube, and a workman taking his life in his hands entered the opening. There were few spectators watching. It was too gruesome and horrible to stand there with the feeling that a slip either way might mean sudden death.

The workman, swathed from head to foot in indiarubber, disappeared from sight. It seemed a long time before he returned, so long that his companions gave him up for lost. Those strong able men who were ready to face any ordinary danger looked at one another askance. Fire, or flood, or gas, they would have endured, for under those circumstances the danger was tangible. But here was something that appealed horribly to the imagination. And such a death! The instantaneous fusion of the body to a dry charcoal crumb!

But presently a grimed head looked out of the funnel. The face was white behind the dust, but set and firm. The pioneer called for lights.

So far he had been successful. He had found the accumulators buried under a heap of refuse. They were built into solid concrete below the level of the tube so that they had not suffered to any appreciable extent.

There was no longer any holding back. The party swung along the tube with lanterns, and candles flaring, they reached the vault where the great accumulators were situated. Under the piled rails and fragments of splintered wood, the shining marble switchboard could be seen.

But to get to it was quite another matter.

Once this was accomplished, one of the greatest dangers and horrors that paralysed labour would be removed. It was too much to expect that the average labourer would toil willingly, or even toil at all when the moving of an inch might mean instant destruction. And it was such a little thing to do after all. A child could have accomplished it; the pressure of a finger or two, the tiny action that disconnects a wire from the live power, and the danger would be no more, and the automatic accumulators rendered harmless.

But here were a few men, at any rate, who did not mean to be defeated. They toiled on willingly, and yet with the utmost caution; for the knots of cable wire under their feet and over their heads were like brambles in the forest. If one of these had given way, all of them might be destroyed. It was the kind of work that causes the scalp to rise and the heart to beat and the body to perspire even on the coldest day. Now and then a cable upheld by some debris would slip; there would be a sudden cry, and the workmen would skip back, breathing heavily.

It was like working a mine filled with rattlesnakes asleep; but gradually the mass of matter was cleared away and the switchboard disclosed. A few light touches, and a large area of London was free from a terrible danger. It was possible now to handle the big cables with impunity, for they were perfectly harmless.

There was no word spoken for a long time. The men were trembling with the reaction. One of them produced a large flask of brandy and handed it round. Not till they had all drunk did the leader of the expedition speak.

"How many years since yesterday morning?" he asked.

"Makes one feel like an old man," another muttered.

They climbed presently into the street again, for there was nothing to be done here for the present. A few adventurous spectators heard the news that the streets were free from danger once more. The tidings spread in the marvellous way that such rumour carries, and in a little time the streets were packed with people.

VII

When the two cyclists came to Deptford, they found that comparatively little damage had been done to the station there, beyond that the offices and platforms had been wrecked. A wounded man was found, who described how a mighty hurricane had roared down the tube ten minutes after the excursion trains had departed. Fergusson made a rapid calculation from the figures that the man supplied.

"The trains must have been near to Park Road Station," he said, "when the explosion occurred. There is just a chance that they may have run into a space free from gas, and that the explosion passed them altogether. Let us make for Park Road Station without delay, and we must try to pick up some volunteers as we go along."

When they arrived at the scene they found that a big crowd had gathered. A rumour had spread that feeble voices had been heard down one of the ventilation gratings, calling for help. Fergusson and Rossiter reached the spot with difficulty.

"Get our fellows together," whispered Fergusson. "We can work now with impunity; and if any of those poor people down below are alive, we shall have them out in half-an-hour. If we only had some lights! Beg, borrow, or steal all the lanterns you can get."

The nearest police-station solved that problem fast enough. A small gang of special experts moved upon Park Road Station whilst the mob was still struggling about the ventilation shaft, and in a little time the entrance was forced.

The station was a veritable wreck; but for two hundred yards the tunnel was clear before them. Then came a jammed wall of timber, the end of a railway carriage standing on end. The timbers were twisted, huge baulks of wood were bent like a bow. A way was soon made through the debris, and Fergusson yelled aloud.

To his delight a hoarse voice answered him. He yelled again and waved his lantern. Out of the velvety darkness of the tube a man staggered into the lane of light made by the lantern. He was a typical, thick-set workman, in his best clothes.

"So you've found us at last," he said dully.

He appeared to be past all emotions. His eyes showed no gratitude, no delight. The horrors of the dark hours had numbed his senses.

"Is—is it very bad?" asked Rossiter.

"Many were killed," the new comer said in the same wooden voice. "But the others are sitting in the carriages waiting for the end to come. The lights in the carriages helped us a bit, but after the first hour they went out. Then one or two of us went up the line till it seemed to rise and twist as if it was going to climb into the sky, and by that we guessed that there had been a big explosion of some kind. So we tried the other way, and that was all blocked up with timber; and we knew then. The electricity was about, and—well, it wasn't a pretty sight, so we went back to the trains. When the lights went out we were all mad for a time, and—and—"

The speaker's lips quivered and shook—he burst into a torrent of tears. Rossiter patted him on the back approvingly. Those tears probably staved off stark insanity. The light of the lanterns went swinging on ahead now, and the trains began to pour out their freight of half-dead people. There were some with children, who huddled back fearfully in their corners and refused to face the destruction which they were sure lay before them. They were all white and trembling, with quivering lips and eyes that twitched strangely. Heaven only knows how long an eternity those hours of darkness had seemed.

They were all out at last, and were gently led to blessed light again. There were doctors on the spot by this time with nourishing food and stimulants. For the most part, the women sat down and cried, quietly hugging their children to their breasts. Some of the men were crying in the same dull way, but a few were violent. The dark horror of it had driven them mad for the time. But there was a darker side to it; of the pleasure-seekers the dead were numbered at more than half.

Rut there was one man here and there who had kept his head throughout the crisis. A cheerful-looking sailor gave the best account of the adventure.

"Not that there is much to say," he remarked. "We got on just as usual for the first ten minutes or so, the train running smoothly and plenty of light. Then all at once we came to a sudden stop that sent us flying across the carriage. We seemed to have gone headlong into the stiffest tempest I ever met. You could hear the wind go roaring past the carriages, and then it stopped as soon as it had begun.

"The rattle of broken glass was like musketry. The first thing I saw when I got out was the dead body of the engine-driver with the stoker close by. It was just the same with the train in front. Afterwards, I tried to find a way out, but couldn't. There was a man with me who trod on some of them cables as you call 'em, and the next instant there was no man—but I don't want to talk of that."

"It means months upon months," Fergusson said sadly.

"Not months—years," Rossiter replied. "Yet I dare say that in the long run we shall benefit by the calamity, great communities do. As to calculating the damage, my imagination only goes as far as fifty millions, and then stops. And yet if anybody had suggested this to me yesterday morning, I should have laughed."

"It would have seemed impossible."

"Absolutely impossible. And yet now that it has come about, how easy and natural it all seems! Come, let us get to work and try to forget."

THE RIVER OF DEATH

A TALE OF LONDON IN PERIL

I

The sky was as brass from the glowing East upwards, a stifling heat radiated from stone and wood and iron—a close, reeking heat that drove one back from the very mention of food. The five million odd people that go to make up London, even in the cream of the holiday season, panted and gasped and prayed for the rain that never came. For the first three weeks in August the furnace fires of the sun poured down till every building became a vapour bath with no suspicion of a breeze to temper the fierceness of it. Even the cheap press had given up sunstroke statistics. The heat seemed to have wilted up the journalists and their superlatives.

More or less the drought had lasted since April. Tales came up from the provinces of stagnant rivers and quick, fell spurts of zymotic diseases. For a long time past the London water companies had restricted their supplies. Still, there was no suggestion of alarm, nothing as yet looked like a water famine. The heat was almost unbearable but, people said, the wave must break soon, and the metropolis would breathe again.

Professor Owen Darbyshire shook his head as he looked at the brassy, star-powdered sky. He crawled homewards towards Harley Street with his hat in his hand, and his grey frock coat showing a wide expanse of white shirt below. There was a buzz of electric fans in the hall of No. 411, a murmur of them overhead. And yet the atmosphere was hot and heavy. There was one solitary light in the dining-room— a room all sombre oak and dull red walls as befitted a man of science—and a visiting card glistened on the table. Darbyshire read the card with a gesture of annoyance:

James P Chase
Morning Telephone

"I'll have to see him," the Professor groaned, "I'll have to see the man if only to put him off. Is it possible these confounded pressmen have got hold of the story already?"

With just a suggestion of anxiety on his strong clean-shaven face, the professor parted the velvet curtains leading to a kind of study-laboratory, the sort of place you would expect to find in the house of a man whose speciality is the fighting of disease in bulk. Darbyshire was the one man who could grapple with an epidemic, the one man always sent for.

The constant pestering of newspaper men was no new thing. Doubtless Chase afore-said was merely plunging around after sensations— journalistic curry for the hot weather. Still, the pushing little American might have stumbled on the truth. Darbyshire took down his telephone and churned the handle.

"Are you there? Yes, give me 30795, Kensington... That you, Longdale? Yes, it's Darbyshire. Step round here at once, will you? Yes, I know it's hot, and I wouldn't ask you to come if it wasn't a matter of the last importance."

A small thin voice promised as desired and Darbyshire hung up his receiver. He then lighted a cigarette, and proceeded to con over some notes that he had taken from his pocket. These he elaborated in pencil in a small but marvellously clear handwriting. As he lay back in his chair he did not look much like the general whose army is absolutely surrounded, but he was. And that square, lean head held a secret that would have set London almost mad at a whisper.

Darbyshire laid the sheets down and fell into a reverie. He was roused presently by the hall bell and Dr Longdale entered. The professor brightened.

"That's right," he said. "Goodd to see somebody, Longdale. I've had an awful day. Verity, if Mr. Chase comes again ask him in here."

"Mr. Chase said he would return in an hour, sir," the large butler replied. "And I'm to show, him in here? Yes, Sir."

But already Darbyshire had hustled his colleague beyond the velvet curtains. Longdale's small clear figure was quivering with excitement. His dark eyes fairly blazed behind a pair of gold-rimmed spectacles.

"Well," he gasped, "I suppose it's come at last?"

"Of course it has," Darbyshire replied, "Sooner or later it was an absolute certainty. Day by day for a month I have watched the sky and wondered where the black hand would show. And when these things do come they strike where you most dread them. Still, in this case, the Thames—"

"Absolutely pregnant," Longdale exclaimed. "Roughly speaking, four-fifths of London's water supply comes from the Thames. How many towns, villages drain into the river before it reaches Sunbury or thereabouts where most of the water companies have their intake? Why, scores of them. And for the best part of a month the Thames has been little better than a ditch stagnating under a brazen sunshine. Will our people ever learn anything, Darbyshire? Is London and its six million people always to groan under the tyranny of a monopoly? Say there's an outbreak of typhoid somewhere up the river between here and Oxford. It gets a grip before the thing is properly handled, the village system of drainage is a mere matter of percolation. In eight-and-forty hours the Thames is one floating tank of deadly poison. And, mind you, this thing is bound to happen sooner or later."

"It has happened," Darbyshire said quietly, "and in a worse form than you think. Just listen to this extract from an eastern counties provincial paper:"

STRANGE AFFAIR AT ALDENBURGH

A day or two ago the barque Santa Anna came ashore at Spur, near Aldenburgh, and quickly became a total wreck. The vessel was piled high on the Spur, and, the strong tide acting upon the worn-out hull, quickly beat it to pieces. The crew of eight men presumably took to their boats, for nothing has been seen of them since. How the Santa Anna came to be wrecked on a clear, calm night remains a mystery for the present. The barque was presumedly inbound for some foreign port and laden with oranges, thousands of which have been picked up at Aldenburgh lately. The coastguards presume the barque to be a Portuguese."

"Naturally you want to know what this has to do with the Thames," Darbyshire observed. "I'm going to tell you. The Santa Anna was deliberately wrecked for a purpose which you will see later. The crew for the most part landed not far away and, for reasons of their own, sank their boat. It isn't far from Aldenburgh to London: in a short time the Portuguese were in the Metropolis. Two or three of them remained there, and five of them proceeded to tramp to Ashchurch, which is on the river, and not far from Oxford. Being short of money, their idea was to tramp across to Cardiff and get a ship there. Being equally short of our language, they get out of their way to Ashchurch. Then three of them are taken ill, and two of them die. The local practitioner sends for the medical officer of health. The latter gets frightened and sends for me. I have just got back. Look here."

Darbyshire produced a phial of cloudy fluid, some of which he proceeded to lay on the glass of a powerful microscope. Longdale fairly staggered back from the eyepiece. "Bubonic! The water reeks with the bacillus! I haven't seen it so strongly marked since we were in New Orleans together. Darbyshire, you don't mean to say that this sample came from—"

"The Thames? But I do. Ashchurch drains directly into the river. And for some few days those sailors have been suffering from a gross form of bubonic fever. Now you see why they ran the Santa Anna ashore and deserted her. One of the crew died of plague, and the rest abandoned her. We won't go into the hideous selfishness of it; it was a case of the devil take the hindmost."

"It's an awful thing," Longdale groaned.

"Frightful," Darbyshire murmured. He was vaguely experimenting with some white precipitate on a little water taken from the phial. He placed a small electric battery on the table. "The great bulk of the London water supply comes from the Thames. Speaking from memory, only the New River and one other company draw their supply from the Lea. If the supply were cut off, places like Hoxton and Haggerstone and Battersea, in fact all the dense centres of population where disease is held in on the slenderest of threads, would suffer fearfully. And there is that deadly poison spreading and spreading hourly drawing nearer to the metropolis into which presently it will be ladled by the million gallons. People will wash in it, drink it. Mayfair will take its chance with Whitechapel."

"At any hazard the supply must be cut off!" Longdale cried.

"And deprive four-fifths of London with water altogether!" Darbyshire said grimly. "And London grilling like a furnace? No flushing of sewers, no watering of roads, not even a drop to drink. In two days London would be a reeking, seething hell—try and picture it, Longdale."

"I have, often," Longdale said gloomily. "Sooner or later it had to come. Now is your chance, Darbyshire—that process of sterilisation of yours."

Darbyshire smiled. He moved in the direction of the velvet curtains. He wanted those notes of his; he wanted to prove a startling new discovery to his colleague. The notes were there, but they seemed to have been disturbed. On the floor lay a torn sheet from a notebook with shorthand cypher; thereon Darbyshire flew to the bell and rang it violently.

"Verity," he exclaimed, "has that infernal—I mean, has Mr Chase been here again?"

"Well, he have, sir," Verity said slowly, "he come just after Mr Longdale. So I asked him to wait, which he did, then he come out again after a bit, saying as you seemed to be busily engaged he would call again."

"Um! Did he seem to be excited, Verity?"

"Well, he did, sir; white and very shiny about the eyes, and—"

"That will do. Go and call me a hansom, at once," Darbyshire cried, as he dashed back into the inner room. "Here's a pretty thing; that confounded American journalist, Chase—you know him—has heard all we said and has helped himself to my notes; the whole thing will be blazing in the Telephone to-morrow, and perhaps half-a-dozen papers besides. Those fellows would wreck the empire for what they call a 'scoop.'"

"Awful!" Longdale groaned. "What are you going to do?"

Derbyshire responded that he was going to convince the editor of the Telephone that no alarmist article was to appear on the morrow.

He would be back again in an hour and Longdale was to wait. The situation was not quite so hopeless as it seemed on the face of it. There was a rattle of wheels outside and Darbyshire plunged hatless into the night.

"Offices of the Telephone," he cried. "A sovereign if I'm there in twenty minutes."

The cab plunged on headlong. The driver was going to earn that sovereign or know the reason why. He drove furiously into Trafalgar Square, a motor car crossed him recklessly, and a moment later Darbyshire was shot out on to his head from the cab. He lay there with no interest in mundane things. A languid crowd gathered, a doctor in evening dress appeared.

"Concussion of the brain," he said in a cool matter of fact tone. "By Jove, it's Dr. Derbyshire. Here, police; hurry up with the ambulance; he must be removed to Charing Cross at once."

II

With no spiritual indigestion troubling him, Mr. James Chase, late of the New York Chanticleer, now of the Morning Telephone, lighted a cigarette at the corner of Harley Street. The night was young and there was plenty of time for him to mature his plans. He had got what he called an "almighty scoop" in his pocket, indeed in the whole history of yellow journalism he could remember no greater. London dried up like a withered sponge and absolutely devoid of water! London with the liquid plague bursting from every subterranean pipe and fountain! The whirling headlines were revolving in Chase's close-cropped head.

He reached the offices of the Telephone at length and crawled up a dingy flight of stairs. Without knocking he passed the barrier of a door marked "strictly private." The controlling genius of the Telephone sat limp and bereft of coat and vest. His greeting of Chase was not burdened with flattering politeness. He merely asked what the blazes he wanted. Chase nodded sweetly and drew a large sheet of paper before him. After a little thought he dashed in half-a-dozen vigorous lines with a blue pencil.

"Things pretty slack lately," he remarked amicably. "So hot that even the East end can't rise to its weekly brutal murder. Still you get on to a pearl sometimes. Grady, my boy, what do you think of that for a contents bill?"

He held the white sheet aloft so that the flare of the gas should fall upon it. The tired look faded from Grady's eyes; he sat up alert and vigorous. Here was the tonic that his fretted soul craved for.

"Chapter and Verse?" he said, speaking fast as if he had run far.

"Got it all from Derbyshire," Chase replied. "I overheard a conversation between him and Doctor Longdale in his own house, Also I managed to get hold of some notes to copy."

"It wants pluck," Grady remarked, "A scare like that might ruin the Empire; if—"

"None of that," Chase cut in. "Take it or leave it. If you haven't got the grit, Sutton of the Flashlight will jump at the chance."

He held the contents bill up to the light again and Grady nodded. He was going to do this thing deliberately, once he was sure of his ground. He remarked cynically that it sounded like a fairy story.

"Not a bit of it," Chase, said briskly. "The plague breaks out on this barque and the crew know it. There's no ceremony with sailors of that class. They just lose their vessel and strike for the nearest land. Knowing something of our quarantine laws they make themselves scarce as soon as they can. A local doctor calls the plague English cholera, too much bad fruit in very hot weather, and there you are."

Grady nodded again. The sweltering heat of the place no longer affected him. Down below the presses were already beginning to clang and boom. There was a constant clatter of feet along the passages.

"Sit down right away," Grady snapped. "Make two columns of it. I'll get some statistics out for you."

Chase peeled off his coat and got to work at once. Grady found the book he required and proceeded to compile his facts therefrom.

The further he dived into the volume the more terribly grave the situation appeared.

The upper waters of the Thames were poisoned beyond doubt. And the Thames for some time past had been little better than a stagnant ditch under a fiery sun. Let that water only find its way into the pipes under London and who could forecast the magnitude of the disaster? Nearly all London derived its supply from the Thames.

So far as Grady could see from a swift examination of Dr. Richard Siskey's valuable book, there were only two London water companies did not derive their stock from the Thames—the New River Company with its 40,000,000 gallons per diem, and the Kent Company with 20,000,000 gallons a day were the favoured ones.

But what of the other six sources of supply? Chelsea, East London, West Middlesex, Grand Junction, Southwark, and Vauxhall and Lambeth were all dependent upon the Thames. Some 250,000,000 gallons of water daily were a matter of necessity for the areas supplied by the above-named companies. Fancy that liquid poison flowing like a flood into the Fast End from Limehouse to West Ham, and from Bow to Walthamstow, and nobody dreaming of the hideous danger! Why, the Great Plague of London would be nothing to it.

And the West End would be no better off. From Sunbury to Mayfair those connected with the Grand Junction supply would suffer. So far as London proper was concerned, only those fortunate ones who were joined to the New River mains would be exempt from peril, and, even then, what chance has a sanitary area surrounded by pestilent districts? If it were not already too late, the only chance was to cut off the contaminated water supply, and then leave four-fifths of the population of London absolutely without water under a heat that seemed to deprive one of vital power.

The further Grady read on the more he was impressed. If he could get this dread information into the hands of the people before it was too late, he felt that he would be playing the part of a benefactor. Desperate as the situation looked, the Telephone might yet save it. Professor Darbyshire had no right to hold up such a secret when he should have been taking measures to avert the threatened danger. It never occurred to Grady that Darbyshire had had this calamity before his eyes for years, and that his genius had found a way to nullify the evil.

"The figures are pretty bad," Grady muttered. "Upon my word, it makes me creepy to think about it. Got your stuff ready? Want anything?"

"Anything in the way of food, you mean?" Chase asked.

"That's it. No? So much the better; because when that copy goes upstairs not a soul leaves the premises till the paper has gone to bed."

An hour later the presses were roaring: presently huge parcels of damp sheets were vomited into the street. Under the glare of the arc lamps perspiring porters ghostly blue and spectral vans waited. The whole street was busy with the hum of high noon. And all the while, a little way beyond the radius of purple arcs, London slept...

London awoke presently and prepared for the day's work. There was no sign of fear or panic yet. A copy of the Telephone lay on a hundred thousand odd breakfast tables, news in tabloid form for busy men to read. As the sheets were more or less carelessly opened the eye was arrested by the scare heads on page 5. Nothing else seemed to be visible:-

THE POISONED THAMES

Millions of plague germs flowing down into London. Bacillus of bubonic plague in the river. New River and Kent Companles alone can supply pure water. Stupendous discovery by Professor Darbyshire. Death in your breakfast cup today. Shun it as you would poison. If you are not connected with either of the above companies, or if you have no private supply.

CUT OFF YOUR WATER AT THE MAIN AT ONCE!

What did it all mean? Nobody seemed to know. At eight o'clock in the morning London's pulse was calm and regular. An hour later it was writhing like some great reptile in the throes of mortal pain.

III

By ten o'clock the authorities had taken the matter in hand. By some mishap the one man who could have done most to help was lying unconscious at Charing Cross Hospital with no chance of his throwing any light on the subject for some days to come. Darbyshire's hurt was not dangerous, but his recovery was a matter of time.

Meanwhile Dr Longdale was the man of the hour. But he could not allay the panic that had gripped London. A deadly fear had taken possession of everybody. Longdale could hold out no hope, he could only give his conversation with Darbyshire and delare that the bubonic microbe had impregnated the Thames. Did he think seriously of the danger? The answer was not reassuring. For his part Longdale would far rather see a million of troops and a siege train battering London than hear of such a thing as this.

There was only one thing for it. It was no time for kid glove remedies. Six of the great London Water Companies had their supply cut off within an hour. It is almost impossible to sit down and realise what this means, and that under a sky like brass and the thermometer at 97 deg. in the shade.

Try and imagine it for a moment, and try and wonder why the thing has not happened before. Think of two-thirds of two millions deprived suddenly of the element which is almost as vital to existence as food. Try and realise that these two-thirds of six millions derive their water supply from an open stream that at any moment by the accident of chance might be turned into a hideous poison-cup.

Under a blazing sunshine after days of heat and dust the packed East-end was suddenly deprived of every drop of water. For an hour or two no great hardship was felt, but after that every moment added to the agony. Before long the railway termini were packed with people eager to be away from the metropolis.

By midday business was at a standstill. There was not a water cart to be seen from Kensington to the Mansion House. Every cart and tank that could be raked together had been despatched into the New River and Kent Water area with instructions to convey a supply as speedily as possible to the congested districts East and South-east of the Thames. By lunch time the City presented a strange spectacle. Well-dressed business men could be seen proceeding in cabs to the favoured area with buckets and water cans with the avowed object of taking a supply forthwith. Cabmen were commanding their own prices.

Fairly early in the morning came the announcement that mineral waters had gone up two hundred per cent. in price. By midday the supply for the time being had ceased. Men of means with an eye to the future had bought up the whole stock. The streets were crowded with people anxiously waiting developments.

For the time being the scare was kept well in hand. What men were most anxious to know, though they dared hardly whisper the question, was whether any disease had broken out as yet. It was a little after two o'clock that the Evening Flashlight settled the question. A boy came yelling down the Strand with a flapping of papers on his shoulders.

"The plague broke out," he cried; "two cases of bubonic fever at Limehouse. Dr. Longdale's analysis. Speshull."

There was a rush for the lad and his papers were gone in a twinkling of an eye. He looked down dazed at the pile of silver and coppers in the palm of his grimy hand.

Yes, there it was right enough. Two cases of bubonic plague had been located in a crowded corner of Limehouse, and Dr. Longdale had been called in to verify them. He had not the slightest hesitation in so doing. Perhaps if the readers of the Searchlight had known these two cases were renegades from the Santa Anna, the panic might have been allayed. But nobody knew.

There was terror in the mere suggestion of the plague. Doubtless, people said, these two poor fellows had drunk of the polluted flood and paid the penalty. But no fever breaks out quite so soon as that and within a few hours nine-tenths of the white-face multitude had drunk of the same stream. Man turned to friend and stranger to stranger with the same dread question in his eye. It might be the turn of any one of them next. There were those who shrugged their shoulders stolidly, others that crept in bars and restaurants and asked furtively for brandy.

The streets were still packed with people waiting for fresh information. By this time there was something like method in the conveyance of water to the affected parts. But after all the New River and Kent companies could not do everything. At the utmost they could supply no more than 60,000,000 gallons per day and now they were suddenly called upon for water for the whole of London. Just enough to drink and keep body and soul together was all that could be expected.

In some crowded districts where great breweries and the like had been established much was accomplished by private enterprise. There were scores of artesian wells in East and South London and these were generously given over at once to the requirements of the people. Even private houses known to possess pumps were besieged and strangers of all classes were accommodated, The situation was dreadful enough but it wouldd be worse if a real panic broke out.

Presently people began to press in dense masses along the Strand and the avenues leading to Trafalgar Square where fountains by Nelson's column were spurting high and clear. There was a continuous rush in the direction of the Square where placards announced the fact that there was no suggestion of contamination here. People danced and raved about the fountain, they fought for the water, they carried it away only to lose it again in the crush, they bent down and lifted the precious fluid to their lips in the hollow of their hands.

Still, there was no sign of panic as yet, no more cases of fever reported. As night fell the streets cleared and something like a normal condition of things was restored.

IV

It seemed indeed as if serious disaster would now be averted. All night long a willing band of firemen and volunteers were engaged in bringing the precious fluid to the famine stricken district. But, including private and other wells, the available supply was little more than 70,000,000 gallons per day and this had to be divided amongst 6,000,000 people over an area of some thirty square miles.

And this, after all, was only a proper precaution. The New River and Kent Companies had a face supply of 50,000,000 gallons per diem, but this was an absolute maximum and far over the average demand.

Moreover, the drought had been a long one, and the reserve reservoirs had been freely called upon. In a day or two the allowance would have to be halved.

Again in the hospitals and sick households water for domestic purposes was absolutely necessary. Meanwhile scores of the main line trains had been knocked off to make way for trains of tanks bringing water from the country. The Spring Gardens officials were working with superhuman efforts.

All night long a stream of people were coming and going between Trafalgar Square and such other open supplies as were available. Morning came at length, with the promise of another sweltering day. A few people turned vaguely to Parliament to do something. Two days before the House of Commons had looked forward to prorogation on Saturday, but there was no talk of that any longer.

The streets began to be busy again. There were smartly-dressed men here and there with grimy chins and features frankly dirty. It seemed strange to see individuals with good coats and spotless linen grimed and lined with the dust of yesterday. A steady breeze was blowing so that in a little time the dust in the streets became intolerable. The air was full of a fine dry powder that penetrated lungs and throat, and produced a painful thirst. It was impossible to water the roads, so that the evil had to be endured.

There was one question on every lip, and that was whether there had been any further spread of the plague. The authorities were exceedingly happy to announce that no further cases had been reported. There was comfort in the knowledge, and London breathed a little easier. Evidently the prompt measures taken had averted all danger of a disastrous epidemic. Gradually it became known who the sufferers were. It was an awful price that London had to pay for the casting away of the Santa Anna.

But that was only the spark to the powder, after all. Extraordinary apathy and criminal carelessness were the causes of the disaster. The knowledge a century hence that London derived its water supply from an open river into which many towns conveyed its sewage will be recorded with pitiful amazement. For the present we have the plain unmitigated fact.

The yellow press made the most of it. The Red Banner pointed to corruption and apathy on the part of the ruling powers; the Red Banner also asked if it were not a fact that our bloated legislators had a private water supply of their own, and that, whilst the common people were allowanced, our law makers were sipping their coffee and tea and whiskey and water as usual?

It was the usual coarse gibe to be expected from a paper of that type, an arrow at venture. But for once the thing was true, seeing that the House of Commons has a private supply of water drawn from a well of its own. As a rule, the Banner carried very little weight, but the question got into the people's mouths and became a catchword. A man had only to pass a standpipe without a struggle in its direction, to be dubbed a member of the House of Commons, i.e., the public want did not touch him at all.

The blazing, panting day wore on. People were beginning faintly to understand what a water famine might mean. Everybody was grimy and tired; in the East and West alike dingy features could be seen. As night fell small riots broke out here and there, people were robbed of their precious fluid as they carried it along the streets. It had leaked out that sundry shops in different parts of London had wells, and these establishments were stormed and looted of their contents by thieves who took advantage of the confusion. It was only by dint of the most strenuous exertion that the police managed to keep the upper hand.

Another day or two of this and what would become of London? At nightfall it became absolutely necessary to release some millions of gallons of the condemned water for the flushing of the sewers. There was danger here, but, on the whole, the danger was less than a wide epidemic of diphtheria and fever. And there were people thirsty and reckless enough to drink this water heedless of the consequences. With characteristic imprudence, the East End had exhausted its dole early in the day, and wild-eyed men raved through the streets yelling for more.

From time to time the police raided and broke up these dangerous commandoes. A well-known democratic agitator came with a following over Westminster Bridge and violently harangued a knot of his followers in Palace Yard. The police were caught napping for the moment. The burly red-faced demagogue looked round the swelling sea of sullen features and pointed to the light in the clock tower. He started spouting the froth of his tribe.

It was all the fault of the governing body, of course. They managed things much better on the Continent.

"If you were men," he yelled, "you'd drag them out of yonder. You'd make them come and work like the rest of us. What said the Banner to-day? Your bloated rulers are all right; they don't want for anything. At the present moment they have plenty of the water that you'd sell your souls for."

"If you'll lead the way, we'll follow," said a voice hoarsely.

The orator glanced furtively around. There was not a single police helmet to be seen, nothing but five or six hundred desperate men ready for anything.

"Then come along," he yelled. "We'll make history to-night."

He strode towards the House followed by a yelling mob. The few police inside were tossed here and there like dry leaves in a flood; the quiet decorum of the lobby was broken up, a white-faced member fled into the chamber and declared that London was in riot and that a mob of desperadoes were here bent on wrecking the mother of parliaments.

An interminable debate on some utterly useless question was in progress, the Speaker nodded wearily under the weight of his robes and wig, the green benches were dotted with members all utterly overcome with the stifling heat. There was to be a big division about midnight, so that the smoking-room and bars and terraces were full of members.

The Speaker looked up sharply. A stinging reproof was on the tip of his tongue. He had scarcely uttered a word, before, as if by magic, the green benches were swarming with the mob. It filled the chamber, yelling and shouting. It was in vain that the Speaker tried to make his voice heard above the din.

A glass of water and a bottle stood on the table before him. One of the intruders more audacious than the rest snatched up the glass and emptied it. A mighty roar of applause followed the audacious act. As yet the mob was fairly good-humoured, though there was no knowing what their mood would be presently.

"It's that confounded Banner," one member of the government groaned to another. "They have come after our private supply. Can't one of you get to the telephone and call up Scotland Yard?"

Meanwhile the mob were inclined to be sportive. They surged forward to the table driving the Speaker back behind the chair, they overturned the table and scattered books and papers in all directions. The foreign element in the company started singing the Marsellaise in strident tones. The martial spirit of it fired the blood of the others.

"We are wasting time here," someone cried. "There are bars and dining- rooms. As we came in I heard the rattle of glasses. This way."

The crowd reeled back as if one motion controlled them all. There was still the same note of laughter in the roar and all might have been well yet, but for the advent of a small, but determined body of police. They charged fiercely into the mob, and in the twinkling of an eye farces gave way to tragedy.

In less time than it takes to tell the police were beaten back with one or two of their number badly hurt, whilst the forefront of the visitors had not come off any better. The popular chamber had become a wreck; outside in the lobby broken furniture was scattered about everywhere.

Then the tide of humanity surged into the bars and dining-rooms. A few frightened attendants and waiters still stuck to their posts. The sight of the glasses and bottles of water about seemed to madden the mob. They demanded that all the taps should be turned on, the fittings were wrenched away amidst a perfect tornado of applause, soon the floors were swimming with the element that all London was clamouring for outside.

The rooms were strewn with broken glass and china, the floors were damp and soppy with the wasted water. Here and there men were feasting on looted food. Never had anything like this been seen in any parliament before. A few courageous members vainly trying to stop the din wondered where were the police.

But they were coming. They did come presently, two hundred of them, steady, stern, and disciplined, and before them the rioters fled like chaff, before the wind. Five more minutes and the House was cleared. But the damage was great.

Outside a dense mass of people had gathered, attracted by the news of the riot. They were in no mood to take the side of law and order and it was with great difficulty that the ring-leaders of the late affray were got away safely. A thin high voice a long way off in the back of the crowd was shouting something which seemed to at once arrest attention. A sullen murmur came up to Palace Yard. The loose jeers of the mob ceased as if by magic.

"What are they saying?" an Irish member asked.

"I can't quite catch it," another member said, "but it's something about water in Trafalgar Square. I shouldn't wonder if—"

Just for an instant the roar broke out again. There was a note of fear in it this time. The babel of voices yelled one against the other. Gradually it was possible to make something out of it.

"By Jove, it's as I feared," the Irish member said. "The spring under the Trafalgar Square fountain has given out. It's a public calamity. See, they are all off. No more row to-night."

The great crowd was melting away with marvellous rapidity. Each man there wanted to verify this new disaster for himself. The mob streamed along towards the Square as if life and death hung in the balance. If fortune had lain there they could not have fought or struggled harder. In the heat and the strife many fell by the way, but they lay there unheeded.

The cool fountain no longer played. People who had come from afar with vessels for the precious fluid cast them on the ground passionately and cursed aloud. The disaster was so great, it appeared so overwhelming that the cruel mood of the mob was held in check for the time. Taking advantage, the police shepherded the mob here and there until comparative quiet was restored. Dr. Longdale, on his way home, paused to contemplate the scene.

"'Blucher or night,'" he murmured, "Darbyshire or morning, rather. I'd give my practice to have a few words with Darbyshire now. I'll just call at the Charing Cross Hospital and see how he is."

It was comparatively quiet in the Strand by this time. Four or five stalwart constables stood on the steps of the hospital as a safe-guard, for there was no lack of water there. A house-surgeon came hurrying out.

"I am very glad to see you," he said. "I was just going to send for you. Dr. Darby-"

"Good heaven, you don't mean to say he is worse!"

"On the contrary, much better; quite sensible, in fact; and he declines to think about sleep until he has seen you."

V

If the-sweltering heat that hung over London added in one way to the terror of the hour, it was not without a beneficent effect in another direction. Under such a sky, and with a barometer somewhere in the nineties, it was impossible for rioting to last long at a stretch.

The early hours of dawn saw London comparatively quiet again. Perhaps it was no more than the sleep of exhaustion and sullen despair, perhaps the flame might break out again with the coming of the day. Down in the East End a constant struggle was maintained, a struggle between the industrious and prudent and those who depended upon luck or the power of the strong arm.

The day came again with the promise of another round of blazing hours. At first there were no signs of lawlessness, nothing more than an eager jostling stream of people pushing impatiently towards the districts where water could be obtained. These were the folks who preferred to get their own instead of waiting for the carts or tanks to visit them.

Naturally, the Press was full of good advice. Thousands of correspondents had rushed into print with many a grotesque suggestion for getting rid of the difficulty. Amongst these ingenious inventions was one that immediately arrested popular attention. The writer pointed out that there were other things to quench thirst besides water. There were hundred of tons of fruit in London, it came up from the provinces by the trainload every day, foreign vessels brought consignments to the Thames and the Mersey. Let the Government pour all this into London and distribute it free in a systematic way.

This letter appeared in three popular papers. The thing was talked about from one end of London to the other. It was discussed in Whitechapel and eagerly debated in the West End clubs.

Instantly the whole metropolis had a wild longing for fruit. Some of the shops were cleared out directly at extraordinary prices. Grapes usually sold at a shilling or two the pound now fetched twenty times their value. A costermonger in the Strand with a barrow of oranges suddenly found himself a comparatively rich man. Towards mid-day crowds began to gather before the big fruit stores, and in the neighbourhood of Covent Garden traffic was impossible.

Prices went leaping up as if fruit had become as extinct as the dodo.

Still the stuff came pouring in in response to urgent telegrams. It looked as if the dealers were bent upon making a fortune out of the public mood. Like lightning the news of what was happening flashed over London, and gradually the approaches to Covent Garden were packed with people.

Presently curiosity was followed by a sullen resentment. Who were these men that they should be allowed to fatten on public misfortune? These things ought to have been given away if only on the ground of mere public policy. Through the crush came a waggon-load of baskets and boxes. A determined-looking mechanic stopped the horses whilst another man, amidst the yells of the crowd sprang to the top of the load and whirled a basket of apples far and wide.

"You've got too heavy a load, matey," he said grimly to the driver.

The man grinned meaningly. He was benefiting nothing by the new order of things. He took an apple and began to eat it himself. In a few minutes every speck of fruit had disappeared.

The thing was done spontaneously and in perfect order. One moment the market had been absolutely crammed with fruit of all kinds, an hour afterwards it was empty.

It was a fairly good-humoured crowd, if a little grim, as yet. But the authorities had serious faces, whilst quite half the police in streets looked shy and out of place as well they might be seeing that several thousand of them had been drafted into London from all parts of the country. Towards midday a sport was added to the amusement of the great mobs that packed the main streets. There was not the slightest reason why all London should not be at work as usual, but, by mutual consent, the daily toil had come to a standstill. It was grilling hot with a sun that made the pavement gleam and tremble in the shimmering haze and there was little to quench the thirst of the multitude. But then did not London teem from end to end with places of public entertainment where thirsts were specially catered for?

Already sections of the crowd had begun to enter them and call loudly for sundry liquids. Why should the hotel proprietors get off scot free? Mysteriously as the sign that called up the Indian Mutiny, the signal went round to raid the public houses. There was no call to repeat it twice.

Everybody suffered alike. The bars were choked and packed with perspiring humanity yelling for liquid refreshment, the men who were wise bowed to the inevitable and served out their stock till it was exhausted and said so with cheerful faces. In the Strand the cellars of certain famous restaurants were looted and one proprietor proclaimed that Whitechapel and Shoreditch had taken from him wines to the value of £30,000. Men were standing in the Strand with strange dusty bottles in their hands, the necks of which they knocked off without ceremony to reach the precious liquid within. For the most part they were disappointed, There were murmurs of disgust and wry faces at the stored juice of the grape that a connoisseur would have raved over.

Fortunately there was little or no drunkenness. The crowd was too vast and the supply too limited for that. And practically there was no rioting where the unfortunate license holders were discreet enough to bow to the inevitable. One or two places were gutted under the eyes of the police who could do no more than keep a decent show of order and bustle about certain suspicious characters who were present for something more than curiosity.

About one o'clock in the afternoon the early edition of the evening papers began to appear. They were eagerly bought up with a view to the latest news. Presently the name of the Mirror seemed to rise spontaneously to every lip. Nobody knew whence it came or why, but there it was. With one accord everybody was calling for the Mirror. There was pregnant news within. Yet none of the papers could be seen in the streets. There was a rush to the office of the paper.

A large flag floated on the top of the building. Across the front was a white sheet with words upon it that thrilled the heart of the spectator.

"The panic is at an end. London to use its full water supply again. Dr. Darbyshire saves the situation. The mains turned on everywhere. See the Mirror."

What could it mean? In the sudden silence the roar of the Mirror printing presses could be heard. Presently the big doors in the basement burst open and hundreds of copies of the paper were pitched into the street. No payment was asked and none was expected. A white sea of rustling sheets fluttered over men's heads as far as the Strand. Up there the turncocks were busy flushing the gutters with standpipes, a row of fire engines was proceeding to wash the streets down from the mains. The whole thing was so sudden and unexpected that it seemed like a dream.

Who was this same Dr. Darbyshire who had brought this miracle about? But it was all in the Mirror for everyone to see who could read.

"Very late last night Dr. Longdale the well-known hygienic specialist was called to Charing Cross Hospital to see Dr. Darbyshire who the night before had been taken to that institution with concussion of the brain. It may not be generally known that Dr. Darbyshire discovered the bubonic plague bacillus in the Thames which led to the wholesale cutting off of the London Water Supply.

"Unfortunately the only man who might have been able to grapple with the difficulty was placed hors de combat. We know now that if nothing had happened to him there would have been no scare at all. Unfortunately the bacillus story found its way to the office of a contemporary, who did not hesitate to make capital out of the dreadful discovery. The dire result that followed on the publication of the Telephone we already know to our cost.

"To obviate that calamity Dr. Darbyshire was on his way to the Telephone office when he met with his accident. Late last night the learned gentleman had so far recovered as to ask full particulars of what had happened and also to see Dr. Longdale without delay.

"Judge of the surprise and delight of the latter to know that matters had been already remedied. It appears that for years past Dr. Darbyshire has been experimenting upon contaminated water with a view to making the same innocuous to human life. Quite recently the discovery has been perfectly and successfully tried with water impregnated with the germs of every known disease. So long as so many great towns draw their water supply from open streams liable to all kinds of contamination, Dr. Darbyshire felt sure there would be no public safety till the remedy was found.

"The remedy had been found and would have been made public directly, when there came the now historic case of the Santa Anna and the alarming outbreak of bubonic fever at Ashchurch.

"On reaching the village in question and on verifying his suspicions, Dr. Darbyshire found that the waters of the Thames were strongly impregnated with the germs of that fell disease. As a matter of fact, the sterilising process was applied at once, and an examination of the water of the Thames a few miles lower down gave the result of absolute purity.

"This part of the story Dr. Darbyshire had no time to tell his colleague Dr. Longdale. He was only too anxious to get away and prevent the issue of a scare leader by the Telephone.

"Accident prevented this design, and when Dr. Longdale was questioned he was bound to admit that he had seen the Thames water strongly impregnated with the bubonic bacillus. After that there was no alternative but to cut off the supply from the Thames. Let us hope the severe lesson has not been in vain.

"Once these facts came to Dr. Longdale's notice, he lost no time. A special train was dispatched to Ashchurch, and returned quickly, bringing specimens of water from the Thames.

"These, after investigation, a small body of leading specialists drank without the slightest hesitation. The new process of sterilisation discovered by Dr. Darbyshire has saved the situation. Otherwise it would have been impossible to magnify the disaster."

Did ever a quiet and dignified newspaper paragraph produce such a sensational outbreak in the history of journalism? Nobody needed to be convinced of the truth of the statement—truth was on the face of it. Men shook one another by the hand, hats were cast into the air and forgotten heedless of the blazing sun; up in the Strand where fire-engines were sluicing the streets with water people stood under the beating drip of the precious fluid until they were soaked to the skin; well-dressed men laved themselves in the clear running gutters with an eagerness that the pursuit of gold never surpassed. London was saved from disaster, and Dr. Darbyshire was the hero of the hour.

The great man was sitting up in bed and modestly listening to the story that Longdale had to tell. Darbyshire was blaming himself severely.

"I ought to have told you," he said. "When I asked you to come round to me the other night I had a dramatic surprise for you. I told you all about the fever and the state of the Thames. From the condition of the germs I knew that the trouble had not gone far. Here was a chance to test my sterilisation on a big scale. I tried it with perfect success. I'll show you the whole process the first time I get back home."

"Yes, do," said Longdale grimly. "It's all right as it is, but if you meet with another accident and another such scourge comes along and we don't know—"

"I quite understand. When I had worked upon your feelings, I was going to show you the whole thing. Then I found out what that fellow Chase had got hold of, and I had to fly off post haste and see his editor. I didn't mind the paper having its 'scare' so long as I came in at the finish with the assurance that there was no need for alarm.

"Hence my hurry, and hence my accident. All the same, it was a mean thing, Longdale. Some day perhaps the country will realise what a debt it owes to its men of science."

Longdale looked at the yelling joyous mob outside heedless of the sunshine and reckless in the hysteria of the moment.

"And perhaps the country will foster them a little more," he said. "Nothing but science could have prevented a calamity that would have multiplied ten-fold the horrors of the Great Plague, and destroyed, not thousands, but tens of thousands."

Darbyshire nodded thoughtfully.

"One of the things that might have been," he said.

"Might have been! We have had a lesson, but I doubt if we shall profit by it. England never seems to profit by anything. It is one of the things that may be. And there is more difference than meets the eye."

FRED M WHITE – A CONCISE BIBLIOGRAPHY

NOVELS (A-Z)

Ambition's Slave (1916)
The Argus Eye (1919)
Blackmail (1902)
The Blue Daffodil (1934)
The Brand Of Silence (1911)
A Broken Memory (1929)
The Bubble Reputation (1908)
By Order Of The League (1886)
The Cardinal Moth aka The Accused Orchid (1903)
The Case For the Crown (1918)
Claxton's Mill (1912)
A Clue In Wax (1930)
The Corner House (1905)
The Councillors of Falconhoe (1922)
Craven Fortune (1904)
A Crime On Canvas (1909)
The Crimson Blind (US title: The Mystery Of The Crimson Blind) (1905)
A Daughter Of Israel (1892)
The Day: Or The Passing Of A Throne (1914)
A Deal In Letters (1923)
The Devil's Advocate (1924)
Dropped From The Fast Express, or A Daughter's Sacrifice (1911)
The Edge Of The Sword (1907)
The Ends Of Justice (1906)
A Fatal Dose (aka Behind the Mask) (1907)
The Fight For The Child (1925)

The Five Knots (1907)
"Found Dead" (1930)
The Four Fingers (US title: The Mystery Of The Four Fingers) (1907)
A Front Of Brass (1910)
The Garden O' Dreams (1909)
A Golden Argosy (1886)
The Golden Bat (1924)
The Golden Rose (1909)
The Green Bungalow (1923)
The Grey Woman (aka Sinister House) (1928)
The Happy Exile (1920)
A Harbour Of Refuge (1918)
Hard Pressed (1910)
The Honour Of His House (1920)
The House Of Mammon (1913)
A House Of Sorrows (1911)
The House Of The Schemers (1906)
The House On The River (1925)
In Trust (1892)
Jim Crowshaw's Mary (1911)
The King Diamond (1927)
Lady Clara (1913)
Lady Edna's Awakening (1920)
The Lady In Blue (1915)
The Law Of The Land (1906)
The Leopard's Spots (1920)
The Lonely Bride (aka The White Bride) (1907)
The Lord Of The Manor (1907)
Love, The Foe (1910)
A Maker of Millions (1909)
The Man Called Gilray (1911)
The Man Who Found Christmas (a novelette) (1915)
The Man Who Knew (1932)
The Man Who Was Two (1921)
The Man With The Vandyk Beard (1925)
The Midnight Guest: A Detective Story (1907)
A Mummer's Throne (1910)
My Lady Bountiful (1905)
The Mystery Of Crocksands (1923)
The Mystery Of The Ravenspurs (aka The Black Valley) (1911)
The Mystery Of Room 75 (1922)
Naboth's Vineyard (1889)
The Nether Millstone (1906)
Netta, The Story Of Sin (1909)
New Century Calendar Clue (1948)
Number Thirteen (1914)
The Old Secretaire: A Christmas Story (novelette) (1887)
On The Night Express (1930)

The Open Door (1907)
Paul Quentin (1908)
Paul, The Sage (1910)
The Phantom Car (1929)
Powers Of Darkness (1912)
The Price Of Silence (1925)
The Psalm Stone (1905)
Queen Of Hearts (1930)
A Queen Of The Stage (1908)
The Riddle Of The Rail (1926)
The Robe Of Lucifer (1896)
A Royal Wrong (1913)
The Salt Of The Earth (1918)
The Scales Of Justice (1908)
Secret Of The River (1934)
The Secret Of The Sands (1911)
A Secret Service (1913)
The Seed Of Empire (1916)
The Sentence Of The Court (1913)
A Shadowed Love (1905)
The Shadow Of The Dead Hand (1926)
The Silver Stream (novelette)
The Slave Of Silence (1906)
A Society Jezebel (1917)
The Sundial (1908)
Tregarthen's Wife: A Cornish Story (1901)
The Turn Of The Tide (1923)
The Weight Of The Crown (1904)
The White Battalions (1900)
The White Bride (aka The Lonely Bride) (1910)
The White Glove (1910)
The Wings Of Victory (1919)
The Yellow Face (1906)

SHORT FICTION SERIES

THE MASTER CRIMINAL (1897-1898)

A series of 12 short stories featuring Felix Gryde, who describes himself as "a really clever soldier of fortune."

The Head Of The Caesars
At Windsor
The Silverpool Cup
The "Morrison Raid" Indemnity
Cleopatra's Robe
The Rosy Cross

The Death Of The President
The Cradlestone Oil Mills
Redburn Castle
"Crysoline Limited"
The Loss Of The "Eastern Empress"
General Marcos

THE LAST OF THE BORGIAS (1898)

A series of stories featuring Professor Victor Colonna, a vigilante physician who murders undesirable people with undetectable poisons.

The Scrip of Death
The Crimson Streak
The Holy Rose
The Saving Of Serena
The Varteg Necklace
The Three Carnations

DRENTON DENN - SPECIAL COMMISSIONER

Drenton Denn is a tough newspaper reporter on the payroll of The New York Post. His hallmarks are a straw hat, a Norfolk jacket, a perennial cigar, and a terrier by the name of "Prince."

The Yellow Moth
The Red Speck
Dust
The Fire Bugs
The Great White Moth

THE ROMANCE OF THE SECRET SERVICE FUND (1900)

This series features Newton Moore, the top agent at The Secret Service Fund.

By Woman's Wit
The Mazaroff Rifle
In The Express
The Almedi Concession
The Other Side Of The Chess Board
Three Of Them

THE DOOM OF LONDON

This sci-fi series of six stories describes a variety of catastrophes which ravage London.

The Four White Days
The Four Days' Night
The Dust Of Death
A Bubble Burst
The Invisible Force
The River Of Death

THE SAGE OF TYBURN (1905-1906)

Each of these stories was preceded by the header The Sage Of Tyburn.

No. 1 - The Chronicle Of The Yellow Girl
No. 2 - The Chronicle Of The Blue-Eyed Syndicate
No. 3 - The Chronicle Of The Inconsequent Princess
No. 4 - The Chronicle Of The Elderly Adonis
No. 5 - The Chronicle Of The Libelled Velasquez

THE DRAGON-FLY (1909)

Six stories about an impecunious but brilliant amateur criminologist, entomologist and ornithologist by
the name of Horace Daimler. Each of the stories was preceded by the header The Dragon-Fly.

No. 1 - How Horace Daimler Got His Name
No. 2 - The Three Red Rats
No. 3 - [title unknown]
No. 4 - [title unknown]
No. 5 - A [illegible] Crime
No. 6 - The Mirror Over The Fireplace

REAL DRAMA (1909)

A series of stories published under the subtitle "Being Some Leaves From The Notebook Of A Late
Theatrical Agent."

His Second Self
An Extra Turn
"Not In The Bill"
The Plagiarist
The Man In Possession
A Pair Of Handcuffs

THE TELEPHONE STAR (1912)

A series of stories about Keith Marrit, a star journalist working for a fictitious newspaper called The Telephone.

No. 1 - The Case Of El Hamid, The Seer
No. 2 - The Case Of The Genuine Counterfeit
No. 3 - The Case Of The Yellow Car
No. 4 - The Case Of Lord Wintercotte
No. 5 - The Case Of The Rusty Nail
No. 6 - The Case Of The One-Eyed Chauffeur

GIPSY TALES (1903-1916)

A series of stories describing the adventures of a wily British navvy with Romany roots, who is known only as "Gipsy." In his fantasies Gipsy portrays himself as a playwright, and tries to stage-manage the dramatis personae and the situations that feature in the stories.

A Matter Of Kindness
A Liberal Education
A Stranger In Bohemia
Drops Of Water
The Unpremeditated Curtain
Mere Details
Out Of Season

THE DIARY OF A LONELY SOUL (1915)

The Diary Of A Lonely Soul - Story 1 [title unknown]
The Diary Of A Lonely Soul - Story 2 [title unknown]
The Diary Of A Lonely Soul - Story 3 [title unknown]
The Diary Of A Lonely Soul - Story 4 [title unknown]
The Diary Of A Lonely Soul - Story 5 [title unknown]

AN A-Z OF OTHER SHORT FICTION

According To The Statute
The Ace Of Hearts
Adventure (aka A Trick of Fate)
After Reynolds
Alias "James Jones"
An Ally
And This Is Fame
Anonymous

The Apple-Green Plate
Applied Mechanics
The Arms Of Chance
Art Critics
At Short Notice
Aunt Mary
Autumn Manoeuvres
The Azoff Diamonds
A Bad Cold
The Balance Of Nature
The Barrister At Bay
Below Zero
The Better Way
Big Fish
The Big Thing
Billy's Xmas
A Bit Of Egypt
The Black Admiral
The Black Cat
The Black Narcissus
The Black Prince
Blind
Blind Chance
The Blindworm
A Block Of Marble
A Bootless Errand
Brayton's Secret
The Broken Lute
A Broken Sceptre
The Broken Trail
The Buff Gauntlet
Burglar Bill's Pupil
By Grace Of His Majesty
By Wireless
A Call On The Phone
A Captious Critic
The Case For The Prisoner
The Charlatan
A Christmas Bride
A Christmas Deputy
Christmas Cards
The Christmas Carol
A Christmas in Peril
A Christmas Star
The Clock Struck Twelve
The Colonel's Christmas Pudding
Compounding A Felony
The Convict

The Gates Of Ramshi
The Grey Bat
The Grey Raider
The Guiding Star
The Half-Crown Princess
The Hand Invisible
Hardy's Big Coup
The Heart Of The Anarchist
Heavy Metal
The Heels Of The Dawn
Her Christmas Dawn
His Christmas Gift
His Majesty's Mails
A Hole In The Net
The Hospitallers
Ice In June: A Playwright's Story
Icky Of Oluk Lake
Imperial Preference
In Black And White
In Rosemary Lane
In The Dark
In The Fog
In The Pit
Introducing Mr. Pentsymon
The Joinville Tunnel
Judgment Reserved
Karma
Kindergarten
The Kingmaker's Token
Lady Mary's Bulldog
The Language Of Flowers
The Last Drive
The Law Of The Jungle: A Tale Of Mean Streets
The Leather-Pushin' Private
The Left Hand
The Lesson The Ants Taught
The Livery Of Death
The Lonely Furrow
The Long Arm Of Bronze
Love In Aether
The Luck Of The Game
Made In England
The Man Himself
The Man Who Got Through
The Man Who Rang The Bell
The Man With The Eyeglass
A Masked Battery
The Master's Voice

A Matter Of Habit
'Merica
A Message from the Flood
The Midnight Call
The Missing Blade
The Missing Note
The Mistletoe Bough
Moray The Traitor
More Than Coronets
The Morning Glory
Music Hath Charms
A Musical Treat
The Mystery Of Room Five
Natural Selection
Nerves
The Night Express: The Story Of A Bank Robbery
The Northern Light
Not On The Records
An Object Lesson
The Odds On Zero
One Day With A Working Ant
One Foggy Night
One Of The Old Guard
On Peace Night
The Onus Of The Charge
The Orpheusia
Ostentation
The Other Man's Story
The Pardon
A Parrot Cry
The Path Of Progress
The Pawn And The Rook
Pearls Of Price
Photo By Lesterre
Pictures In The Snow (a Christmas story)
A Place In The Sun
The Platinum Chain
A Popular Novelist
Poste Restante
A Prize Crop
Proof Positive
The Purple Terror
A Queen In Hiding
A Question Of Money
Rachel's Seventh Year
Rawhide Science
The Real Dramatic Touch
A Record Round

Red Petals
Rob Peter—Pay Paul
A Rope Of Snow
Rose Of The Desert
A Royal Bag
The Royal Train
The Salmon Poachers
Santa Anna
A Satisfactory Reference
Saviour From The North
The Second Chapter
Second In The Field
The Shebeeners
A Single Hair
Sir Jeremiah's Big Shoot
Sister Louise
The Sixteenth Chapter
A Sleeping Partner
Sleeping Partner
A Sound In The Night
"Special" To The Telephone
A Stolen Interview
The Straight Game
The Stranger Within The Gate
Sub Rosa
The Substitute
The Superman
The Supreme Test
The Sword Of Justice
A Table Tragedy
The Thirty-Seventh Month
This Little World
A Thrilling Exit
The Throat Of The Wolf
The Ticket
To Be Let Furnished
Treasures Three
The Two Bon-Bons
Two Of Them
The Unbelieving Eye
Unbidden Guests
The Unexpected
An Unrecorded Crime
The Vital Spark
The Vital Spot
War Ribbons
The Waterwitch
The Western Way

When The Moon Set
The White Geranium
The White Spot
White Wings (1922)
The Wings Of Chance (1922)
The Witness (1920)
The World Next Door (1916)